♥ Emily Gale ♥

Girl, ALOUD

Chicken House

2 Palmer Street, Frome, Som

Of course the characters in this book only hear Simon Cowell as an imaginary voice in their heads. We are not quoting from any actual TV programmes or any real dialogue.

Text © Emily Gale 2010
First published in Great Britain in 2010
The Chicken House
2 Palmer Street
Frome, Somerset BA11 1DS
United Kingdom
www.doublecluck.com

Emily Gale has asserted her rights under the Copyright, Designs and Patents Act, 1988, to be identified as the author of this work.

Cover and interior design by Tracey Paris
Cover illustration Jerry Paris
Typeset by Dorchester Typesetting Group Ltd
Printed and bound in Great Britain by CPI Bookmarque, CRO 4TD

The paper used in this Chicken House book is made from wood grown in sustainable forests.

5 7 9 10 8 6 4

British Library Cataloguing in Publication data available.

ISBN 978-1-906427-20-7

To Madeleine and Jonah, who are much better at waiting than I am.

Chapter One

A Game Show Host Ate My Dad

Who wants to be . . . a million miles away?
I do. [Drum roll]
Ladies and Gentlemen, it's Saturday night!
Time to play . . .
Who Wants To Be A Millionmilesaway?
And here is your host . . . **My Dad!**
[Weak applause]

Thank you, thank you, thank you. Yes, I'm Her Dad.
Welcome to a very special edition of . . .
   Who Wants To Be A Millionmilesaway?
   Let's crack on with the first question. Contestant
Number One, for a hundred miles: what is this model
family-of-four having for dinner tonight?
   For a brief but precious moment I forget that I
know the answer – all the answers, in fact – to all the

questions in the very disturbing pretend game show that goes on in my head when real life gets too tragic. With parents like mine, we're On Air pretty much every day.

The answer to the pretend question for a pretend one hundred miles is on the small round table that the contestants are sitting at (the game show host is standing by the oven): four plates, four glasses, four white paper napkins, no knives or forks.

– Umm, I'm gonna go with C: Pizza. Pepperoni and mushroom, times two, reheating in the oven against the advice on the box – but I can tell you now that nothing bad happens if you eat reheated pizza because we do it every Saturday night. Without fail. And we're all still here. Unfortunately.

– It IS pizza! You're on your way to being a million-milesaway!

– I wish. Can we just eat now?

– All in good time! Second question: for two hundred miles – what's for pudding?

The set of *Who Wants To Be A Millionmilesaway?* looks a lot like an eat-in kitchen; the host even wears oven gloves. We film on location at 127 Mallow Lane, deepest, darkest, dorkiest suburbia. It's so pristine in here Ikea could photograph it for their catalogue, but they'd have to move the contestants out of the way because we're much too funny-looking. Especially me and Dad.

The lighting is on the slightly painful side of bright, because the game show host likes to see what he's eating. (Living under a flight path as we do, I think we can assume that there are people on planes who can see what we're eating.)

The round table is protected by a vinyl tablecloth with a red apple pattern. The apples are all identical, and shiny, and the kind of vivid red that is probably supposed to make you feel like skipping through an orchard. I once used a black marker to draw a little worm peeking out of one of them, but Mum (a.k.a. Contestant Number Two) killed him with one squirt of Cillit Bang.

One of the apples hanging down the side has a massive cigarette burn in it. *That* wasn't me.

— *I'm going to have to press you for an answer here.*

— *Hmm, it's a toughie. Could it possibly be A: Your homemade pineapple upside-down cake, famous for its chewiness, as in, like a mattress?*

— *Is that your final answer? You could ask the audience.*

— *Audience? No one watches this show. It's rubbish. The answer is A.*

— *Right again! You've won two hundred miles AND this delicious reheated slice of pizza! Next question: what does this family do after dessert?*

The game show host takes a seat next to me – grinning and fidgeting, oblivious to the bright orange pepperoni juice smeared across his cheek. The other contestants chew like robots. In fact there's more going on *under-neath* the table.

The legs swinging opposite mine, not close enough to be called kicking but near enough to create a rhythmical wind that scuffs my jeans, belong to Contestant Number Three: my brother Raff. He is a small-time criminal, a master of deception. On his lap is a personal organiser – sorry, 'BlackBerry'. Dad's current favourite gag is to call it a 'Plum'. Last week it was a 'Strawberry'. Can you see where this is going? How many fruits are there in the world? That's how far he'll take it.

The grubby fingers that are not above the table holding reheated pizza are typing speedily but silently. This is one of Raff's many talents that go unnoticed, along with lock-picking, pickpocketing, eBaying stolen goods and credit card fraud. He is thirteen.

The legs to my right are perfectly still; the feet look glued together at the ankles, in shoes I haven't seen before – black with a small heel. Slim legs in beige stockings; the skirt just comes to the knee. This is Contestant Number Two: Grace. My mum.

Strange how, to everyone else, she was Grace before she was a mum, but to me it seems the other way round.

You can't be called Grace and just get away with it; people expect things of you – grace, for a start, and with that a soothing voice, a light touch, a delicate beauty . . . an immaculate Cillit Bang-ed kitchen, smooth hands with manicured nails that never get pizza topping stuck underneath them, quietness, shiny hair, the kind of face that makes you sigh and immediately catch sight of your own, much larger, nose. That may seem like a huge burden for a one-syllable name, but it's true. This particular Grace ticks all the boxes.

The legs to my left can't stop moving. One foot shuffles, the other taps, completely out of time with each other. They stop and the movement travels up the legs, making them jiggle. Stop. Shuffle-tap-jiggle. Stop. Shuffle-tap-jiggle. The legs are hyper. They wear new jeans, trendy ones; the feet are in Nike trainers, so fresh from the box you could get high on the smell of rubber. If you had to date the legs you'd say they were in their twenties. Why can't they just be normal like other dads' legs?

He's so twitchy today it's possible he'll spontaneously combust, but I suspect this strangeness is going to lead to something much more damaging. *For me.* It always does when he's like this.

That just leaves my legs – they're on the chubby side of ordinary, and fifteen years old. There is nothing else to say about them.

– *The answer's B: Play Pictionary.*
– *You're sure? Remember, you can phone a friend!*
– *My two best friends are at the cinema together having a nice time like normal teenagers do on a Saturday night.*
– *You'll thank me in years to come for this quality family time – it's healthy!*
– *It's killing me.*

— Haha! Come on, now, I'm supposed to do the jokes! OK, for a thousand miles: what's going to happen next?

So this is us; this is how we are. In a second, Dad will jump up and collect the plates, sprint to the kitchen and put them in the oven. He won't eat reheated pizza off cold plates, so between slices he reheats the plates along with the pizza and we all sit there with nothing to do but *ting* our nails against the glass water jug (Mum), type more quietly than the hum of the fridge (Raff), and wait for the quick-fire round of questions (me).

'How was school?'

'Fine.'

'Any tests?'

'No.'

'They don't test enough these days. Any essays back?'

'No.'

'What's *wrong* with these teachers?'

Shrug

'Don't worry, Kassidy, Dad's got your future all mapped out.'

I hate it when he refers to himself in the third person. But for a quick-fire round that was really tame. He's not letting anything get to him tonight – this is what it's always like on his first day back. Back from where? The simple answer would range from 'bed' to 'armchair' to 'bath', as those are the only places you'll find him when he's not being one of the two other Dads he's got in him: Vaguely Normal and On The Up, as he likes to call it, as if that's a good thing. It's basically a frying pan or fire situation.

'Kassidy-Kassidy-Kassidy,' he says, using a different facial expression each time he says it, the way you might do *in private* when you're testing out how to say hi to a cute boy. 'Kassidy Kennedy.' He traces imaginary words in the air and looks deep into La-la Land. 'Oh yes, oh *yes*, you're in safe hands, my love.'

Great. One of those safe hands is now reaching into the back pocket of the trendy jeans. It pulls out a packet of Marlboro, the strong kind.

'Just time for a quick one before the next batch!' He winks at Mum, she smiles serenely, Raff smiles sarcastically, and I lay my head on the apples and sigh. We all watch him exit the patio doors with his toothy theatrical grin. You'd think living with a person that excitable would whip everyone else up, but when he's like this I just feel done in.

The night air that comes in when he goes out makes us shuffle in our seats. Mum clears her throat and tells Raff to eat his crusts. Raff ignores her and types two-handed.

'Can we watch *X Factor*?' I say.

'Well . . .'

'It's on in five minutes.'

'No, then. You know Dad likes us to sit together on Saturday evenings. And this is the first day he's been . . .' She doesn't have to say it. *Back*. She means his mind, obviously.

'But it's the final.'

She gets up and goes towards the oven. Useless.

'Not yet!' says Dad, and he's in and across the room like a gazelle. He hops a bit from foot to foot in front of the oven door, rubbing his hands, and Mum returns to her seat. Raff's still typing without looking, though he now puts one hand on the table.

'Just stop it,' I whisper at Raff as the wind-scuff against my jeans becomes too much to bear.

'Stop what?' he whispers back, flapping his legs even harder. I move my chair back a little, hoping that my restraint will annoy him in some small way. I feel like doing something – anything – to stop this from being the dire Saturday night game show it's destined to be, just so I don't know what's going to happen before it does, just so I can't guess every thought in every person's head (except Dad's, which could do with some profes-sional head-reading, let's face it) or every reaction to every single predictable word spoken.

And then Dad does it for me.

'Let's take this lot through to the other room,' he says, and all three of us turn our heads towards him with the kind of speed that could cause whiplash.

'Huh?' says Raff. He has actually stopped typing.

'Pardon?' says Mum. I just stare open-mouthed at the figure of my father edging towards the kitchen door under the weight of four reheated plates and two reheated pizza boxes.

'I want us to watch *X Factor*,' he says, as if that's a perfectly normal thing to announce after years, literally *years*, of us never being allowed to watch Saturday night television for fear of ruining the tradition of the four of us – including whichever version of Dad happens to be present – eating reheated pizza around the round table in our kitchen.

Nobody speaks. Until I do.

'*Why?*' I say, doing nothing to hide my deep suspicion. Dad smiles, the kind of smile that lets me know that there is much, much more to this than I want to know. He doesn't break traditions for nothing.

'They'll be starting a new series of *X Factor* soon,' says Dad.

Oh.

God.

No.

'And guess who *I* think should be at the front of the audition queue!' It's not a question. He disappears with his load as my chest begins to thud so loudly I'm sure I'm having some sort of heart attack. He's come back from The Dead to deliver my invitation to Personal Hell. Mum gives me a sympathetic look and touches my arm lightly as she says, 'Well, you did say you wanted to watch it this evening.'

'Yeah, you did say that, Kass.' Raff is loving every minute of this. He's even put his organiser away.

'I wanted to watch it, not *be* on it,' I say, practically hissing. This is serious. This is big. He's finally lost it and he's taking me with him.

Game show: OFF AIR.

Chapter Two

Dad Digs A Really Big Hole, And I Jump In

I lurk in the doorway while the rest of them get comfortable. Dad leaps in front of the telly like a paunchy ballet dancer, remote in hand. He turns ITV on but presses the mute button, and then he announces:

'I've been thinking.'

Here we go. My dad + thinking = very bad thing. In the past, my dad + thinking has equalled:

– *Kassidy should join Mensa!* (international high IQ society)

– *Kassidy is entering a chess tournament!*

– *I've put Kassidy on the books of a child modelling agency!*

– *Kassidy* must *try out for the National Youth Orchestra!*

And now watch him transform from wonderful,

supportive parent to deranged, embarrassing idiot when we look at the rest of the facts:

– *Kassidy's IQ is so low that . . . she doesn't even know what IQ stands for.*

– *Kassidy only remembers the name of one chess piece. A prawn, isn't it?*

– *Anyone can go on the books of this child modelling agency (for £250).*

– *Kassidy barely scraped Grade 2 clarinet. Even then, she suspects, her dad bribed the examiner.*

(I hate it when I think about myself in the third person.)

But I could go on. When I say it doesn't take much to get Dad:

'Thinking'

I mean that I've become so self-conscious about my:

'Talents'

that I've even developed an unattractive walk. Seriously. He will pick up on anything when he's On The Up.

'What the audience of this show *loves* is the Wild Card. The one who starts off at the back, but somehow steals our hearts.' He doesn't just *say* these words, he *performs* them. It's nauseating.

'And,' he whispers, looking cheekily from Mum to Raff and then to me, 'her voice isn't half bad either!'

I quickly rewind back over the last few days until I remember Dad clapping like a seal in my bedroom doorway, where he'd obviously been standing for some time to watch me applying mascara while singing something (out of tune) from my KT Tunstall album. That was the spark. *THAT*. It's like watching me brush my teeth and telling me I should be a dentist.

I can't sing.

I can-NOT sing.

Glued to the doorframe, I am still taking all of this in. I've been here before and it hasn't ended well, for anyone. I don't want to say a single word until I am sure my words will be convincing enough, but all I can think of so far is:

Help!

I want my insanely dull Saturday night back; I promise never to complain about reheated pizza and pineapple upside-down cake again.

'*You've* got the likeability factor, Kassidy,' says Dad.

'The *what?*' says Raff.

'It's what Simon says. Likeability. It's even more important than having a good voice – and Kassidy has *got* it.'

My brother comes over to me.

'*This* Kassidy?' he says. 'Err, she only has *two* friends. How is she likeable?'

He's right, but I'd still like to hit him.

'Raff, if you've got nothing sensible to contribute . . .' Dad wags his remote with a stern look on his face, and Raff takes a seat with his hands in a prayer position as if we've just been doing judo, an impish grin on his face.

Mum is doing her nervous throat-clearing thing. As usual, she's choosing to ignore what's going on. Well, it's not as if Dad's On The Up mood affects *her*.

Dad un-mutes the telly, and he and Raff chew pizza and grin at each other like happy pigs eating from a trough. My dad is too dense to realise that Raff is laughing *at* him, not with him. Raff knows that when Dad is occupied with a grand plan for me, the spotlight isn't going anywhere near him for a long time, and that can only mean: *kerching!*

Mum pats a space next to her to beckon me in.

'Come on, it's just the ads now,' she says. But as I sink into fake leather I see I've been duped.

'If YOU want to audition for the next series of The X Factor, *here's what you need to know.'*

My dad knees his way towards the television with half a slice of pizza in his mouth and a pad and pen in his hands.

Band members and solo artists must be aged sixteen or over to enter—'

'Ha! See?' My voice is so excited I sound like I've inhaled a helium balloon. 'Aged sixteen, aged *SIX-TEEN*, did you hear?' Bottom-bouncing on the sofa is probably not a good look but I'm very, very happy. It's over! I'm saved!

But wait, why is Dad shaking his head, revealing a smug smile oozing with pizza?

'Dad? What is it?' He looks like a demonic four-year-old whose parents are about to discover that he's crayoned all over the plasma telly.

'Passport,' he says, into his chest, trying to hide his grin. 'I know a bloke who knows a bloke who . . .'

'You can't be serious! So now you're turning me into a criminal? No way.'

'Yes way.'

How can I debate reasonably with a thirty-nine-year-old who still uses the noway/yesway tactic? I need new ideas, and fast.

'Dad, think about it – people always get found out when they lie about their age on these shows. Why not just wait a year or two until I'm old enough?' (As in, old enough to leave home, change my identity and live peacefully on a small island earning a living making useful things out of coconut shells – *anything but this*!) 'Plus, Dad, look at me – I don't look sixteen.'

Raff comes over, snarling in the direction of my chest. 'S'true. She's got no boobs, look.'

I gasp and cross my arms over my chest, and try unsuccessfully to punch him in the head with my elbow. Dad roars: 'Rafferty! Stop looking at your sister and go have another slice of pizza.'

I hate to agree with my brother – on anything – but he has a point. Plus I know how much my dad hates talking about things like "boobs". I might be able to embarrass him into submission.

'Raff's right, Dad. They're flatter than fried eggs.'

'Enough,' he says. 'No more talk of . . . them. I've got to think.'

'You've done enough thinking,' I mumble. He takes another huge bite of pizza.

'I've got it,' I think he says, though it's slightly muffled until he swallows. 'We'll say you've been poorly.'

'Paul!' Mum hardly ever 'Pauls' him; at least it's not just me who thinks he's finally lost his one remaining marble.

'That's not *getting it*,' I say. 'That's the opposite of getting it. I'm not "poorly", Dad, I'm just fifteen. And tone-deaf. Game over. The End. Let's just turn it off and play Pictionary.' (You know things are desperate in this house when someone volunteers to play a competitive game with Dad in the room. Especially Pictionary. Especially when he's like this. We could end up with extravagant doodles all over the wallpaper, like Rolf Harris on a caffeine high.)

'This is your twist,' he says. 'Everyone needs a twist on this show – a gimmick, something that people will remember, maybe even make them feel sorry for you.' Dad gets up and paces the room as if he's solving a crime. As a matter of fact, this *is* a crime, with several charges: passport fraud, entering a competition under false pretences and child cruelty, for starters. But Dad will never point the finger at himself.

'Dad, people will remember me for being rubbish. You know this – you make me enter karaoke every year on holiday and I never, *ever* fail to suck!'

He is chewing pizza so quickly it's made him profoundly deaf. I try again.

'Anyway, saying I'm ill isn't a twist, it's a lie.'

'It's terrible,' says Mum, but much too quietly to have any effect.

'It's brilliant! Your likeability and my sales skills . . . come on, you lot, you know I could sell lard to Victoria Beckham! I'm on the up!!'

Affirmative. He's in another world. And I'm in hell. Suddenly he jabs his pepperoni slice in my direction.

'Sing us something, Kassidy. Come on, just a few bars.' He tries to get me up and over to the mantelpiece using bare enthusiasm, as if I'm some half-witted Andrex puppy. 'She's good, Grace, she's really improved.' My mum smiles at him. *Don't* smile at him, that'll just encourage him! 'This is it,' he says, clenching his fist as if he's just discovered a way of turning house dust into gold.

He's too far gone for me to argue. It could make him worse; he's not like other people. I feel awful saying that. It's not that I've completely forgotten all the ways that he can be amazing like other dads don't seem to be – like the spur-of-the-moment holiday to Florida, or the day he got his ear pierced with me because I was scared to do it on my own – but lately it feels like he needs *Handle With Care* tattooed on his forehead.

I need help, and I'm not going to get it in this room. If I protest any more he'll list every sales job he's ever had and every dream sale he made, starting with the Famous Bag Of Manky Cooking Apples (circa. 1979) and not forgetting the time he shifted three washing machines to the same person (well, *I'd* buy three washing machines just to make him *GO AWAY!*). Or Worse, and believe me, there is a Worse. It's not the kind of Worse you can get locked up for, but it's the kind you don't invite to parties. It's the kind nobody really talks about.

I've got to get out of here.

'Actually, Dad, I've got a bit of a tickle in my throat. Better save my voice, don't you think?'

From the look on his face you'd think I said *terminal*, not *tickle*. He clamps my shoulders meaningfully between his hands and looks into my eyes. Then he runs from the room and the rest of us wait in limbo. When he returns it is with a glass of cloudy liquid, which he stirs frantically, not noticing the small spills on his trainers.

'Here, drink this.'

'What is it?'

'Salt water. The professionals use it.'

I look at Raff, who cannot conceal his joy.

'That's right,' Raff says. 'Britney uses it.'

Dad snatches the glass from my hand.

'But she's ruined herself,' he says to Raff. 'Two young children and all that rehab for that, umm, whatever it is she's got.' We all go deathly silent, and there's only the sound of the spoon clinking around the glass. He looks at the drink as if salt water were directly responsible for Britney's downfall. Raff nods and says:

'True, but I also heard that Kylie drinks it.'

'Really?' Dad's face lights up again. He stops stirring and passes the drink back. The temptation to throw it over my brother is huge – he doesn't have to put up with any of this unwanted attention and all he can do is gloat – but I've got to play the long game here. This is no time for rash actions.

I cough a little and put my hand to my throat as if I'm in pain. It's lame, but it works.

'I'd better have this upstairs and then get some rest.'

'Yes, yes, off you go, Kassidy.' As I'm walking away he's saying, 'Good name for a pop star, isn't it?' And Raff is agreeing and Mum is silent, of course.

I trudge up to my refuge with a glass of spew. Dad's still bouncing around and I can barely put one foot in front of the other. How can someone being that happy make me feel this bad? But here's the irony. This is how we *all* prefer Dad – by a whisker – because when he's not acting like this he's being something completely different; and you really, really don't want to know.

The decision of whether to call Izzy or Char is made for me when I look at the time: nine-thirty. There are probably all sorts of reasons I don't know about why most of my friends with divorced parents are allowed to take calls later, but this doesn't apply to Char's house (probably because her dad is still massively in denial about her mum walking out). So I'm dialling Izzy even though I'm more in the mood for Char (but definitely not in the mood for Char's dad giving me a lecture on the proper time to use the telephone). Besides, Char seemed a bit stressed out last week, which isn't like her, so she probably doesn't need me laying a whole bunch of anxiety on her shoulders. By contrast, Izzy will ask for seconds. She's an issues junkie.

There are good points and bad points to knowing someone as long as I've known Izzy. BAD: she knows all the really embarrassing stuff that's happened to me. GOOD: she knows all the really embarrassing stuff that's happened to me, and she's *still* hanging around. But sometimes I wish I could have kept it all to myself, kept the conversation about normal things, like GHDs instead of GTDs: that's Dad's Grey Tracksuit Days, which usually turn into Grey Tracksuit Weeks, and recently even into Grey Tracksuit Month which, at the end of last year, was about the worst thing that's ever happened to this family. It coincided with Dad finding out that I'd secretly resigned from the Debating Society at school, and a big row we had about my future. Mum must have said 'It's not your fault' about a hundred times. She's a terrible liar.

The trouble is that while the GTDs happen behind closed doors, when Dad's On The Up there aren't even carbon steel armoured doors with patented locking system that could contain him (don't ask how I know about those). He's truly Out There.

Because my night/life is already ruined, I'm not a bit surprised when it's Izzy's mum who answers the phone. She's a therapist. The therapist is in therapy. The therapist's daughter is in therapy. The therapist's ex is a lawyer, and he's not in therapy, but the therapist and the therapist's daughter, who's in therapy, think he should be. Talking to Izzy about her family is guaranteed to give me either a headache or a lisp.

'Hi there, Kass. How are you feeling?' The way she says *feeeeling* is clearly meant to be very *soooothing*.

'Really great, thanks, Mrs Franklin – I mean, *Doctor* Franklin!' I try to sound like I've just got off the best fairground ride ever, so that she doesn't ask me to lie down on her imaginary couch.

'It's Barbara, darling, please.' (I know it is, and we've had this conversation about once a week since I was little.)

'OK, sorry, Barbara! May I—'

'Are you sure you're all right, Kass? You sound a bit—'

'No, I'm *really* great, thanks. *Barbara.*'

'How's school, then? Izzy never tells me anything.'

I am really tempted to suggest that Izzy's mum should ask Izzy's therapist how school is, as Izzy readily admits she tells her therapist *everything*.

'It's really great.' I know I sound as if the fairground high has worn off a bit, but I'm too exasperated to bother now. *I don't want to speak to you, Barbara! Please put your daughter on, Barbara!*

'And how's the family?'

'Fine. Really fine. Is Izzy back from the cinema, *please*?' Great, now I sound like the fairground ride has turned my stomach and I'm desperately looking around for somewhere to chuck.

'I'll just get her.' She sounds really put out that I didn't want to chat more. Yuck. I feel bad enough when I upset my own parents, let alone someone else's.

'Hi, it's me. What's happened, Furbs?' Izzy sounds very grown-up and serious, although she's still managing to call me by the pet name I loathe beyond all loathing (I may have neglected to tell *her* this). *Apparently* I used to look like a Furby. It was a long time ago and my hair now covers my ears.

'It's my dad.'

'Oh. I saw him earlier. He had loads of shopping bags.'

'Yeah, he went out and bought all these clothes he's much too old for.'

'Oh, *God*. My dad did that when he turned forty, except he bought a Porsche and went out with a teenage stripper.'

'Izzy, she was in her late twenties and she worked at the Carphone Warehouse.'

'Yeah well, whatever. Count yourself lucky.'

'Sure, remind me to count myself lucky when I'm standing in a mile-long queue waiting to SING in front of SIMON COWELL.'

'*What?*'

'That's what he wants me to do.'

'Who? Simon Cowell?'

'My dad!'

'Oh. But, Furbs, you can't really sing – not being mean or anything. You can do tons of other things.'

'I know I can't sing, Izz. You don't have to tell me that.' Hearing her say it does sting a little, even though I know she's right. I stop speaking for a moment to give her room to list the things I *can* do . . .

Izz? Got any examples?

Silence.

I almost wish I'd risked it and called Char. She spins sympathy like a spider spins silk – she'll wrap you in it like a cocoon, and even though you know you can't stay in there forever, it feels really good while you do. Izzy's into realism and cold, hard truths.

'You're too young! Simple. He's not going to go as far as breaking the rules,' she says.

'He's going as far as breaking the law, Izz. As in getting me a fake passport.'

She gasps: 'Seriously?'

'Yes – I never thought I'd make it to a young offenders' institution before my brother.'

'Well, just say *no*, then.' Sometimes for a trainee therapist she can be very simplistic.

'You *know* that doesn't work on my dad.'

'Right, hmm. Is he still having those episodes?'

'What "episodes"?' I can hear the extra harshness in my voice, and my heart is beating really loudly now that Izzy has said that. *Episodes? It's not* Hollyoaks. *It's my dad.*

'Don't get stressed, I just mean that your dad has some undiagnosed . . . well, *I* know the term for it but you don't like to talk about it so . . . come to think of it, doesn't he always buy a whole load of new clothes when he starts a new cycle?'

'Oh, does he? Well, thanks, Doctor, I'll pass that on.' I don't want to feel this mad with Izzy but I can't help it when she gets like this. *I'm* allowed to talk like that about Dad, but it hurts too much when she does. As soon as anyone else is mean about him it unlocks the musty old room in my brain that stores all the good stuff about Dad.

Half of me knows that Izzy is still talking, but the other half is remembering the summer I turned twelve. It was the day before a new school year and we'd spent the whole summer away – Dad had sprung it on us. He'd collected Mum from work, Raff from primary school and then me. 'Get in! We're going to Florida!' I can remember the look of amazement on Izzy and Char's faces as we drove away with Dad still shouting out about our plans through the car window. *His* plans. He'd packed all our stuff; no questions asked, he'd thought of everything. It was like being in a film – a whole summer of Disneyland and the beach and swimming with dolphins. Unreal.

But then we were back home and I'd confessed that there was an important school project due in the next morning. It was supposed to be about 'Something Everyday That We Don't Know Much About'. I'd let myself forget all about it, but now I felt sick with how stupid I'd been and couldn't face going to school empty-handed.

'You can still do it, Kassidy,' said Dad.

'Dad, don't be ridiculous,' I said. 'There are only twelve hours between now and school and I don't even know what the project is going to be about!'

Mum had been hovering in the kitchen doorway.

'Tea, anyone?' she said.

'Brilliant!' said Dad, jumping up. It was the most

over-the-top response to an offer of tea anyone had ever seen.

'It's just tea, Dad,' I said.

'Ah, but it's not, is it? It's your project, Kassidy! Something Everyday That We Don't Know Much About. TEA! Come on, we can do this.'

'We?' I said.

But he was already flicking through his phone book, muttering something about a bloke who worked for PG Tips owing him a favour, and before I knew it the sitting room had been transformed into Operation Help Kassidy. By seven o'clock in the morning (hours after I'd fallen asleep with a pen in my hand) I had the weirdest and most brilliant project on tea ready to hand in.

Dad slept for two whole days after that. I can't remember what happened next, which usually means it wasn't good. I only got a B+ but I didn't tell him that.

Now I tune back in to what Izzy's been saying.

'Look, Furbs, he can't actually *make* you audition. It's cruelty to children. Simon Cowell is the original mean judge – for years they've used him to clone other mean judges.'

'Yeah, I know! It'll be a bloodbath. TV's Mr Nasty meets a tone-deaf banana. But there's nothing I can do.'

'You have rights. You're not his puppet.'

'Oh yeah? Remember the Captain Birdseye thing?'

'God, yes. Oh, Furbs. Poor you.'

And just like that we're in the other room in my

brain – the much bigger room, which is full of all the *other* stuff about Dad.

Picture three children in the hallway of a small Victorian house. The two girls are aged eight (the one who isn't me looks at least ten), and are trying desperately to ignore the boy, who is six and wants to show them his top score on Tetris.

'Just buzz off.'

'But look how good I am.'

'Daaaaaad, Raff's annoying us, are we going yet?'

The dad springs down the stairs. He is wearing a look that makes one of the girls feel a teensy bit suspicious, though she isn't old enough or jaded enough to recognise this look as 'very sheepish'.

'Are we going to Alton Towers now?' she says.

'Everyone in the car!' he says, ushering the three of them out the front door with the cheesy enthusiasm of a game show host.

On the road, the taller, serious-looking girl whispers to the other:

'I don't think this is the way to Alton Towers.'

''Course it is,' says the other girl, who sometimes finds her friend a bit of a know-it-all.

Half an hour later the car stops in front of an old theatre.

'I told you,' whispers the know-it-all friend. The other girl shushes her – she still eighty-per-cent believes that her dad has brought them to Alton Towers, though this looks nothing like the pictures she's seen on telly.

Inside the theatre, the dad speaks to a lady who gives

him a number and makes a tick on her clipboard. The dad pins the number to the girl.

'Does this mean I can go on the rides?' she asks.

'This way!' says the cheesy game show dad. There's a stage, and on it is a line of children. One by one they go over to a table, at which is sat an old man with a white beard who is dressed in naval uniform.

'You're late,' says a woman with very glitzy glasses and a stern suit and another clipboard. She uses her chin to point violently towards the back of the queue on stage, and then she looks at the front of the queue and shouts: 'NEXT! OK, for the last time the line is: *Only the best for the captain's table.*'

She is very scary; so scary that the girl's left knee starts to give way when she's walking down the aisle towards the stage, as the dad is pushing her to do. And he's whispering to her . . . *You just need to say one line . . . just do what they tell you . . . try to be natural . . . smile . . . I just know you're going to do brilliantly . . . make your dad proud, eh?*

She is *still* clinging onto the twenty per cent of her that thinks the dad has brought her to Alton Towers. But the percentage begins to fall as she climbs the stairs onto the stage and joins the line of girls, and looks back at the know-it-all friend and the annoying little brother and the beaming dad.

And then she feels dizzy – what was the line again? – and then she feels something quite warm trickling down her leg, and into her sock. She is frozen to the spot, and all she can see is the dad's big cheesy set of teeth. But as the girl next to her starts to nudge her a bit, she sees the smile disappears into his mouth, and she can hear someone saying 'wet herself', and all the muscles that were holding up her dad's expression seem to collapse, and then she can hear someone saying 'For God's sake get her off', and the dad is holding his hand out but not looking at her, helping her back down the stairs and up the aisle to where the know-it-all friend and the annoying little brother are standing with their mouths wide open and something in their eyes she will later recognise as pity.

Phew. It still makes me nauseous just thinking back to that day. The audition – my first, sadly not my last – was for a TV ad for Captain Birdseye's Fish Fingers. As if! Like I'd want to advertise something as grim as ground-up fish bits in a bright orange crispy coating. I don't want to advertise *anything* (except perhaps my need for a new dad).

I cried the whole way home, not just because I'd wet myself in front of dozens of people, but also because Izzy had tried to warn me that we weren't really going to Alton Towers and I hadn't listened to her – I'd even been cross with her for doubting my dad. But most of the tears were for the look on Dad's face. Even after he'd lied to me and humiliated me, *I* still felt like I'd let *him* down.

Izz breaks into my thoughts. 'Are you still there, Furbs?'

'Yeah, sort of,' I say.

'I'm sure Mum's got a leaflet on this in her surgery.'

'No thanks.'

'Right. Do you want my help or not?'

'Not really. I just called you as a friend, not as a shrink.'

This always happens. Why do I never learn? I should have kept this private, only it seems to affect so much of my life that if I kept it *all* to myself I'd have nothing to say, ever.

'*Maybe* you really do want to enter,' she says, teasing me. '*Maybe* the lady doth protest too much, methinks.'

'Yeah, well, *me*thinks you should shove that copy of *Hamlet* up your bum.' (We're doing it for GCSE – not shoving it, just reading it.) 'Anyway, how was the cinema?' I change the subject and my tone because it's getting too much, and Izzy's not helping, though I know she'd like to. I'm grateful she doesn't run a mile, I suppose, after all the weird behaviour she's witnessed in this house.

I make sure we have a good chat about normal things and then I make my excuses and tell her I'll call her tomorrow.

Afterwards I lie down on my unmade futon and close my eyes.

– Hello, sweetheart, and what's your name?

– It's Kassidy. I mean, Kass, Kass Kennedy. Sorry, Mr Cowell.

– OK, Kass-Kass Kennedy, what makes you think you've got the X Factor?

– It's just Kass, Mr Cowell.

– Right. Just Kass. So, what makes you stand out from the rest?

. . .

– Anything?

. . .

– Anything at all? – come on, sweetheart, we're filming here.

– I'm just really ordinary, Mr Cowell. I'm normal.

– Great. Fabulous. Just what we're looking for. Right, says here you're eight years old.

– No, I'm . . . errr . . . sixteen.

– It says eight here. You must be mistaken. And what are you going to sing for us today?

– 'Suddenly I See' by KT Tunstall.

– Mm. It's not very 'young', is it? Do you know any other songs?

– No, just that one.

– Ugh. OK then, go ahead if you must.

. . .

– I said start.

. . .

– Darling, if you're not going to sing, you're just wasting my time.

– Sorry, I'll do it now.

– Fine.

– Only the best for the captain's table!

– Pardon?

– ONLY THE BEST FOR THE CAPTAIN'S TABLE!

– Oh God, have you just wet yourself? Security, get her out of here.

– But listen, I've really got it now:

ONLY THE BEST FOR THE CAPTAIN'S TABLE!
ONLY THE BEST FOR THE CAPTAIN'S TABLE!
ONLY THE BEST FOR THE CAPTAIN'S TABLE!

Chapter Three

He Might As Well Stand At The Front Door With A Sawn-Off Shotgun

Sunday mornings should be sacred. I don't mean religion; I mean that I should be able to walk downstairs wearing an old, stained hoodie and tracksuit bottoms and with mascara smudged under my eyes without running into a pervy thirteen-year-old who looks at me as if I'm Mischa Barton at a premiere.

He's enormous compared to the Miniature Terror I call my brother – the same height as me, how irritating – since when did Raff's ankle-biting friends hit puberty? This one even has tiny bits of black fluff sprouting from his chin, but it looks more like dirt than stubble. He also has alarmingly pink cheeks and bulging eyes; a sort of giant furry clowny toad. This is typical; no one normal could ever fancy me.

'Hey. I'm Lucas. Luke.' The voice is like someone's first go on a violin, but it's pretty brave of him to introduce himself. It's as if he's been doing a flirtaphone tutorial, like the kind people use to learn French. I look at Raff, sitting cross-legged in front of the Wii, but he is oblivious to this revolting attack.

Now the Toad is looking at me as if I'm ice cream. *Shiver* Isn't he a bit young for hormones?

'Hi, Lucas, *Luke,*' I say, trying to sound as unappealing as I can by mocking his little intro. Dad comes in from the kitchen, wiping his hands on a tea towel. His outfit + his bounciness = there has been no Return To Planet Earth overnight.

'Morning, love. How's that throat? You sound a bit croaky. Didn't the salt water help?' He wipes his hands harder and looks me all over as if he's checking for a rash. The Toad takes this as his cue to come closer and do the same.

'Are you ill, Kass?' says Toady.

'No.' I pull my hood up over my head to scowl inside. Who *is* this brat?

'Are you cold?' says Dad, and he goes to put the tea towel around me.

'No! Can I just sit down?' They both make room for me to get to the sofa, and gawp as if any minute I'm going to morph into a rare yellow-tailed woolly monkey and start swinging from the light fitting. Finally I'm saved by Raff.

'Luke, are you playing or what?'

The Toad reluctantly joins him.

'What can I get you for breakfast?' says Dad.

'Just tea, Dad. Thanks.'

'Eggs? Porridge? Bran flakes? You should have some fibre.'

'How is fibre going to make me a better singer?' I already want to cry. I wish I'd never come downstairs.

'OK, OK, I don't want you getting upset. Tea, then.' On his way into the kitchen he passes Mum as if she's a pillar in the way instead of a person; she looks at him – but I can't work out what the look is – and smiles an *oh-well* smile at me as she takes a pile of folded towels upstairs. She mouths *Morning*. I scowl; it's not really meant for her but for my general situation.

In my sleepiness I become transfixed on what Raff and Lucas are up to.

'I'll put 50p on Brazil, with an extra 10p for Ronaldo to be the top scorer,' says Lucas.

'I can give you odds of 7/1 for Brazil and 3/1 for Ronaldo,' says Raff, consulting a small red notebook. They are both speaking out of the sides of their mouths in hushed tones and looking around shiftily. This is like watching *Bugsy Malone*. Any minute now they'll break into a rendition of 'We're The Very Best At Being Bad'. Lucas nods and they shake hands, clumsily exchanging coins as they do. Raff reaches under his fleece top and pulls out a black drawstring pouch. Who does he think he is now, Shylock?

'What about the other bet?' says Lucas, bending nearer my brother. Raff catches my eye for an instant.

'Not now, later.'

'Err, what's going on?' I say.

'Nothing, Mariah,' says Raff.

'You'd better not be betting on me, you little rat-face.'

'Don't flatter yourself, Christina Aquilera.'

'Don't be a wanker, Raff,' says Lucas. Wonderful: a thirteen-year-old over-fizzing with hormones is my only supporter.

'Thanks, Lucas, I can stick up for myself if you don't mind,' I say.

'Sorry, Kass.' His wounded puppy look is no more appealing than his lovesick gaze. 'Anyway, Raff, it's Aguilera. My mum's got her album.'

'Who cares?'

'No one. Shut up.'

'*You* fucking shut up.'

My dad pops his head into the room and for a second I think he's going to pull Raff up on swearing, but like all Raff's sins it goes unnoticed and Dad just gives me the thumbs-up sign, bobs around and pouts his bottom lip. Then he puts the tea towel over his head and swings it like it's dreadlocks. It's a shame I'm not three years old or he'd have really cheered me up by now.

The doorbell rings.

I wouldn't usually be up first to answer; especially not on a Sunday morning, dressed like a vagrant and still caked in yesterday's face. It barely registers when Lucas says, 'That'll be my brother.'

'Hi, is this the Kennedys'? I'm Cass.'

'Huh?' The weather that comes through the door is

cold enough to burn, but that's not what's making me freeze. There is some kind of demi-god standing at my door; well, either that or not washing your mascara off at night can profoundly warp your eyesight.

'I'm Cass. I'm Lucas's brother.'

'Oh. Hi.' Is this how one addresses a demi-god, I wonder?

'He's here, isn't he?'

'Yeah, he is, yeah.'

There is a pause. A tiny part of me knows that the pause is because I'm checking him out from head to toe, but that tiny part is unfortunately located in a dormant part of my brain.

'Well, I've come to fetch him,' he says, in that sweet, deep way of his. (Already he has a 'way'.)

Suddenly the door is pulled back behind me.

'Let him in, you idiot,' says Raff. 'Hi, Cass.'

'Oh, sorry!' I say, and giggle, and squeak slightly when The Other Cass catches my little toe with his big brown boots. He didn't mean it, obviously. He just has really, really big boots, and my stupid toe was in the stupid way.

'I'm called Kass, too,' I say but my voice seems to have disappeared inside my unwashed, saggy tracksuit bottoms and he doesn't hear over the noise of canned football cheering.

'What's the score, boys?' he says. He crouches down and puts his hands on the bases of their necks affectionately.

'One-nil to Brazil.'

'Which one of you is Brazil?'

'Me,' says his brother, beaming at The Other Cass. Lucas gets a head-ruffle and I feel awful for being so mean to him before. When he's not perving on me, he looks like quite a sweet kid.

I stand there behind The Other Cass and ponder his tousled hair, the colour of dark chocolate. Would it be so very wrong to go over and smell it? Suddenly I realise he might be able to see my reflection gawping in the television.

'Did you want tea or something?' I say. I think I've crossed and uncrossed my arms a dozen times since he walked in. I've also made three resolutions:

I am never getting up late again.

I am never going to bed in make-up again.

I am never being mean to dear sweet Lucas again.

The Other Cass gets up and wanders away from the boys and towards me slightly, sideways, keeping an occasional eye on the screen. What, my just-got-out-of-bed look isn't utterly captivating? Amazing.

Dad shouts from the kitchen: 'Are you sure you don't want eggs, Kass?'

'I'm sure, Dad,' I shout back. The Other Cass looks really confused (and yet still remarkably sexy). 'Kass is my name, too,' I say. 'Well, Kassidy, but only my dad calls me that, I don't actually like it, so I'm just Kass, like you.' Somebody switch me off, quick.

'I'm Cassian.' He offers his hand, and a cheeky grin. I just about manage not to giggle when I shake it. I notice how clean his fingernails are – not like most boys

I know – most of the boys I know being Raff's friends. (I haven't quite made it to the dating scene I hear so much about – hey, I've been busy having my entire life ruined by my dad.) He seems about twenty years older than any other boy I've ever spoken to – in a good way. Hand-shaking? Being nice to little brothers? Those enormous brown boots? And don't even get me started on his eyes (green). We've barely spoken and already I'm starting to obsess. I expect it will all come undone soon enough; usually does.

'So, you go to St Agatha's?'

'Yes, how did you know?'

'Not sure, I think Raff told me.' My heart plummets: if Raff talks about me to hand-shaking boys in brown boots, it's almost certain he knows all my warts already – actual and metaphorical. I have an actual one right now on my elbow. It's *hugely* unlikely that he can see it under the stained hoodie but I put my hand over it anyway.

'Where do *you* go?' I say, hoping not to sound like a stalker.

'Dudley College. Know it?'

Never heard of it. I nod vigorously.

'What are you studying, Cass?' I can't say his name without smiling and I don't think I've ever been more aware of my teeth. I feel like a very nervous horse.

'A whole bunch of 'ologies,' he says. 'Nothing interesting.' I'd beg to differ, only I've heard the begging look is not that attractive. 'Hey, who's the stamping guy I passed on the way here?'

'Oh, that's the Stamping Man,' I say, immediately wishing I hadn't announced it as if he were a fairground attraction.

'So I almost got his name right.'

I don't know what to make of this. He's smiling at me but I feel really stupid.

'Um, yeah. Well, he stamps. A lot. For hours, actually, in the same spot. He's done it for years. It's weird because he's really well-dressed. But we don't normally walk that way.'

The Other Cass kind of nods and smiles, but I'm sure behind that smile he is deeply unimpressed.

'Here we are, Kass. Sorry I took so long – stewed the first one while I was checking something out on the internet for the audition.' There's a faint buzzing in my left ear that I really hope is a pesky fly and not my peskier dad.

'Morning, Mr Kennedy,' says The Other Cass.

Damn, so it *is* my dad. And now he's shaking hands with The Other Cass, and all I can think is that I never want these two people to be in the same room, especially if I'm also in it. While they exchange niceties I edge my way to the staircase. As much as I want to be near Brown Boots for a bit longer, even if he's going to crush my little toe again, I can't take the risk.

'Kass, your tea!'

Double damn.

'Great, thanks. Mmm, yummy.' *Yummy?* Am I five years old, and is this a cup of fairy cakes covered in sugar strands?

'So what's this audition on the net?' says The Other Cass.

'It's nothing,' I say with lightning speed, narrowing my eyes at Dad, who is, of course, looking in the opposite direction.

'It's for *The X Factor*,' says Dad. The Other Cass laughs, though not in an obviously unkind way.

'Go for it, Mr Kennedy!'

'Oh, it's not for me; it's Kass here. She's very talented.'

'I'm not; I'm *really* not.' This is hopeless. 'Anyway, nice to meet you. Bye.'

It's a terrible idea to leave my dad talking to a lovely hand-shaking boy in brown boots with the same name as me, but it's on a par with having to witness the event. That's settled, then: I will die an Old Maid.

'Seeya. Good luck. Sounds cool,' he says.

Ugh. I'm heartbroken already. I haven't even got the strength to turn back round and thank him.

It's at times like this that I remember why I chose the room at the top of the house. Most people focus on the bad points:

1. There is almost no floor space, what with my bed, wardrobe, desk, and collection of Desperate Dad gifts designed to bring out the high achiever he's convinced is buried underneath my ordinary skin, that have achieved precisely nothing except for accumulating a layer of dust over the years (the easel, the electronic keyboard, the cello, the surfboard . . .).

2. There is almost no space above my head in the middle of the room, and the sloping walls mean that I've had to develop a semi-permanent stoop.
3. There is almost no light.
4. There is even less air.
5. It is almost certainly a fire risk.

But I wouldn't change it for the world. Even the constant cooing that seeps through the roof day and night doesn't bother me. I'm sick of everyone picking on pigeons, anyway. When we moved here, Raff thought he'd get one over on me by giving me the nickname Pidge and trying to make it catch on.

'Pidge lives up in the roof. Cooo-cooo,' he'd say, in a high-pitched birdy voice, whenever someone came over. I really didn't mind – suits me better than Kassidy, or even Kass, which I manage to insist on to everyone but Dad – but Dad put a stop to Pidge.

Up here, I can almost forget about down there. Up here, they don't seem *so* bad. Usually. Take Raff (please, someone take Raff) – even he has his good points. Sometimes I lie awake at night and try to remember what they are. Once I came up with: *he has a phobia of chickens*. I know that doesn't sound like a good point exactly, but it's a weakness, and believe me, any chink in that boy's armour is something to be cherished.

He'd have been seven or so when he first developed a habit of sneaking frozen food up to his room and sucking on it like ice-lollies. It was mainly peas, sometimes sweetcorn, but one day he took a chicken breast and devoured the whole thing while playing one-handed FIFA. He was so, so sick. The next time Mum served chicken, he made a distressed baboon noise and before we knew it chicken was banned in the house. Mum insisted, which isn't like her, but when it comes to Raff's wellbeing she seems to manage it. Dad and I even had to stop sneaking out for a crafty McChicken Sandwich on Saturdays because, three hours later, Raff could still 'sense' it.

But enough of his good points. The first indication of Raff's absolute lack of morals burst in with a fanfare when he drowned one of my dolls in the bath. He can only have been four. After that her eyes never closed, as though she had to remain permanently awake in case he came for her again. Sometimes I'd widen my eyes like hers and try not to blink for as long as possible. Awful. To say that from that day forth Raff has embarked on a systematic destruction of my personal happiness, and that I have eyed him with mistrust ever since, would be totally precise.

Perhaps the most teeth-grindingly annoying thing about him is that he never gets caught. His crimes seem to pass people by ('people' being Mum and Dad). They don't know he smokes cigarettes, they don't know that he's driven the car at least twice in the middle of the night (that I know of, and I've got better things to do than be on his case all the time, so it could be hundreds of times), and they *definitely* don't know that he's dabbled in Class C drugs. It's not as if I've never tried to bring it to their attention. But somehow I've never

been able to make it sound true. I always end up looking like a liar. Motivation: just being a pain-in-the-butt
big sister, Mum reckons.

Someone knocks lightly on my bedroom door. It
isn't Dad. He used to just barge in, until the day Mum
and I went out shopping and came home with my first
bra. Now he does a hefty *rap-ra-ra-rap-rap*-pause-*rap-
rap*, and waits for me to open it myself, and he always
looks around the room before getting on with whatever
he's come to say, as if he's worried about what frighten-
ing piece of teenage girl paraphernalia might jump out
at him.

It isn't Raff. He doesn't have a knock, exactly, but a
series of irritating noises: a dull whistle through the
keyhole, or an unconvincing *coo*.

So, by a process of elimination . . .

'Come in, Mum,' I say.

She pokes her head around the door.

'How did you know it was me?'

I shrug and go over to my stereo to put on some
background music.

Mum comes all the way in, closes the door and
stands just to the right of it, craning her neck. She looks
more like she's come for a job interview than a mother–
daughter pep talk.

'Did you want something?' I say, probably more
curtly than I should have, judging by the injured look
on her face.

'I just wondered how you were.' She goes to sit on
my unmade futon, lowering herself smoothly instead of

flopping down like any normal person. 'This is nice, what's this?' She means the music.

'Just a song I thought I'd practise for my audition.' I stare at her until she realises that I'm being sarcastic. Her mouth nervous-twitches into a weak smile, and she tries to pull her skirt over her knees but it won't go.

'I had no idea he was planning this,' she says, to the carpet.

'I know.'

Dad announces things, he doesn't ask for opinions. There's never any warning about what mood he's going to be in, either, only we know that On The Up can last for weeks on end, but the GTDs usually don't last the month. Except for last time.

'You know what he's like,' she says.

'Yep.' This is us having a deep and meaningful.

'It's only because he's proud of you, Kass. He believes in you. We're not all so lucky as to have that kind of . . .' Her voice trails off. She has a habit of not finishing her sentences.

'I don't *feel* very lucky.' There's a burning sensation in my throat telling me that I need to nip this conversation in the bud unless I want a grand-scale scene on my hands. Izzy and Char are always asking why I never try to get Mum on my side to help me fend off Dad when he's cooking up something horrifying to ruin my life. All they see is this beautiful, calm, rational, *nice* woman, and she is, but I can't rely on her for disasters like this. Dealing with Dad's GTDs saps all her energy and there's nothing left for me.

At least I don't have to worry about her making things worse; I just wish I could rely on her to make things easier. I know she used to make me feel better – plasters, cuddles, hot Ribena – but I need something a bit stronger now.

'It's just that doing this for you makes him so . . . happy,' she says, as if 'happy' is a word like 'cancer' or 'AIDS' that people like my mum find really awkward to get out. We stare at each other until she looks away, and now there is something so heavy between us it's as if the figure of Dad hunched over on the floor, lost in one of his darkest moods, is right between us.

I'm not stupid – I can see why Mum would want me to just get on with it instead of kicking up a fuss. Right now Dad's on Planet Up, which orbits yours truly and means that everyone else gets a holiday. For me, Dad's 'happy' isn't exactly infectious. (At least, I hope not.)

'Isn't it nice that he believes in you,' she says, not quite a question but a statement. 'Look, you don't want to end up like me.'

'Why, what are you that I don't want to end up like?'

'Well, I'm a slave in that office, you know that. And *here* I'm . . . well, I'm your mother and that's wonderful, but . . .'

But? I know she'd never say the but.

'I don't see why it has to be a choice between slave and pop star,' I say. 'Slave or top soap actress. Slave or renowned scientist. Slave or the actual Queen of England. Why is it always extremes? What about all the things in between?'

'I know, Kass. I just . . . look, we both know how difficult Christmas was and I think this is a *good* sign, overall. We don't want to . . .'

It's as if her brain short-circuits the minute she's about to say something heavy.

'We don't want to *what*? Make him barricade us in again, or obsessively Google carbon steel armoured doors with patented locking systems while he rapidly smokes himself to death? *What*?'

Mum turns her face as if I've just slapped her, and I grab a discarded jumper and bury my face in it. It stinks of Dad's cigarettes.

'Kass! Let's not do this now. Don't upset yourself any more. Please.' It looks like this meeting has adjourned. Then she gets up with that same fluid motion, stoops to come nearer to me and puts her hand on my shoulder. I flinch and feel guilty all at once, but I just can't let myself get upset in front of her, otherwise I'll start to want things from her that I know – while I'm still slightly rational – that she won't be able to give me.

'OK, sweetheart,' she says. She's *so* forgiving. 'I'll leave you in peace.'

She closes the door with the care of someone trying not to wake a baby.

Peace? She thinks she's leaving me in *peace*? As soon as she's gone I throw down the jumper and start to pull fistfuls of my hair to the millisecond before it feels like a layer of my scalp will peel away. I have to think, I have to plan, I have to get myself out of this. My scalp aches and I breathe deeply and sit cross-legged on the floor, head in hands.

It's not self-deprecation to say that I can't hold a tune; it's called having ears. My voice hovers somewhere between tone-deaf and almost bearable if singing very quietly.

But this isn't as simple as queuing up in the cold, singing half a bar, thanking the judges for their comments and going home. This is My Whole Entire Life for the next few weeks – eating, sleeping, breathing, talking non-stop *X Factor*. This means no going out, no having friends over. This is Dad pouring every ounce of energy into something he believes in more than most people believe in gravity, which means there is a whisker of a chance that he might somehow, *somehow*, get me past the first round and into boot camp. It would be nothing to do with me and everything to do with him if that happened, but he has his ways – he'll wear them down if nothing else. He is a salesman and I am a bag of manky cooking apples!

And whenever I fail, which I always do (without fail), we have to go through the whys, and I feel like a dead body in the morgue being picked apart. This is followed by a range of conspiracy theories that are less reasonable than alien landings. And afterwards, even though it signals the end and I should be thankful, there is that moment when he realises that it's really over, and the look on his face. It is not a simple look; there are layers to it.

Then there's the next morning: the feeling of dread as I walk downstairs, searching Mum's face for a sign that he's OK, he hasn't slipped into another bad cycle. You just never know.

Izzy reckons Dad's easy to feel guilty about because he has lots of childlike qualities. She knows a lot of stuff like that because she's been in therapy for two years over her parents' divorce. But I hated it when she said it, as if she were looking down on Dad.

Not all of Dad's qualities are childlike anyway; some of them are just plain weird. For example, Dad's favourite film is *National Velvet*, which is about a little girl who pretends to be a boy so she can win a horse race. As if it's not bad enough that he can't like something normal and dad-like, he actually quotes lines from it when my friends are over: 'Some day you'll learn that greatness is only the seizing of opportunity, clutching with your bare hands 'til the knuckles turn white.' And he actually makes fists till the blood drains away and holds them up for everyone to see. When you have a dad like that, you can tell who your real friends are by the people who show up a second time.

Even our names are down to his conviction that what we're called determines who we are or how successful we'll be. That's why he nipped Pidge in the bud. (*'My daughter, a common pigeon?'*) Wait for it . . . Kassidy means *clever*. Which is stupid. First, it's stupid because the word Kassidy does *not* *sound* clever at all. Second, I'm not. I'm OK; I'm average. I know this because in a class of thirty pupils I come fifteenth in every single subject on just about any occasion, except if someone is off sick, and it doesn't take a genius to work out how average that is, it takes someone of *average* intelligence. Me.

I might not be up to much in the IQ department, but surely I can ease my way out of this stupid audition. I've just got to go about it gently – back away without any sudden movements.

Rap-ra-ra-rap-rap-pause-*rap-rap*.

Speak of the devil.

'Yes, Dad, come in,' I say, with all the enthusiasm of a cold, wet sponge.

'Everything all right?' he says.

'Actually, no, Dad, I'm not doing it.'

OK, I seem to be going for the direct approach instead.

'Excuse me?'

'No.'

'No?'

'I said no, I do not excuse you for interfering in my life *again*.'

'Don't speak to me like that, I'm your father.' Our voices rise in volume a little more with each sentence.

'Right, so as my father, why don't you respect what I want?'

'You don't know what you want, Kassidy.'

'I do!'

'Oh yes? Please tell me, then.'

'Why should I?'

'Now you're being a baby. I know what's best for you. And it's not boys, before you start getting any ideas.'

'I'm fifteen, Dad, you can't make me do things like this any more.'

'Come on, Kassidy, I'm not *making* you. I do all this for you, you must understand that.' He starts to go red in the face and shaky. 'I never had parents who believed in me like I believe in you.'

Shit. Why does he have to do this? It's like he's the only one who's allowed to feel *anything.*

'What, you mean they actually let you make your own decisions?' I say. He slams the door and I jump a little.

'*You* don't know what . . .' He stops. He's out of breath and his eyes are about as wide as they could get. He's right; I don't know what they were like. We've been Here before – and when I say Here, I mean this awkward pause just before Dad *might* tell us something about his past, because as far as we know he came into existence some time in his twenties, when he met Mum.

He takes a deep breath and gently opens the door, as if he can undo the slamming. When he next speaks he's calm again.

'I don't ever want you to feel like you're not good enough, Kassidy; to have someone wreck your dreams. I've made the most of what little I had, but for you there is so much more.'

Inside I am screaming at him: *But these aren't my dreams! These are* your *dreams! I don't want more; I don't want fame.* It is *too much* that it is up to me to wipe that tragic look off his face. But I know that this is not going to be the time that I get through to him. I'm not totally spineless – I've said no before; I regretted it. *Everyone* regretted it. There has to be another way out.

'Actually, Dad, I'm just getting dressed, so . . .'

'Yes, yes, of course. I'll go. Don't be mad at your old dad.' He hunches up with his hands in a begging position and alarmingly reminds me of Gollum. I can't like him because he keeps messing up my life, but I can't hate him either. And I shouldn't pity him, should I?

I'm fifteen and I can't even stand up to my dad. One more fail.

Chapter Four

All I Want For Christmas Is A Carbon Steel Armoured Door With Patented Locking System

For the rest of the day I'm locked in my room. When I say locked, I really mean that I've wedged a flip-flop under the door so that entry will be slow, if not impossible. Dad won't let us have proper locks on our bedroom doors. Which is ironic.

Luckily I can survive on emergency rations:

 – last night's by-the-bed water (complete with mysterious bubbles);

 – the Rolo that Char taped onto a home-made Valentine's card last year . . . or possibly the year before;

 – a pear from my school bag (apart from the gross bit imprinted by my spiral-bound notebook);

 – an entire packet of tortilla chips that I blackmailed

Raff to fetch for me by sending him a text to say that, yes, I had noticed that he'd recently eBayed three of Dad's DVD box-sets.

In between snacking I've been staring at the computer screen, hoping that the blank Word document will miraculously fill up with sentences that form an A* essay entitled: *Discuss examples of ways in which Willy Loman's suicide is foreshadowed in the first act of the play.* Not that I ever got an A* in my entire life, or possess the power of telekinesis. It would probably help if I read the play, or if I could ever bear to have the book face up on my desk instead of hidden under a magazine and a packet of face wipes. *Death Of A Salesman* – just a little too close to home what with my dad being (a) a salesman, and (b) let's not go there. When the book first got handed out in class I skipped to the notes at the back so I already know that it's about the *actual* death of an *actual* salesman, not just the death of his career, which I suppose would be quite a boring play and not exactly a 'tragedy'.

Eventually I stop pretending I can ever hope to concentrate on the essay and fully commit to buying one from Raff later (another secret and profitable line of his, which not even Izzy and Char know I take advantage of). I check my email approximately once every thirty seconds until something comes through from a random person on Facebook who friended me weeks ago saying she was Char's cousin's friend from junior school.

Rachel Olsen has invited you to take the WHAT MENTAL DISORDER DO YOU HAVE? quiz. C'mon, we know you must have something!

I get a lurch in my diaphragm that very nearly gives the tortilla chips an encore, and delete the email. I know it's random and she probably sent it to another fifty people, but it *feels* personal. Now I'm stuck with a bouncy voice inside, saying: *We know you must have something!*

I don't. I don't have anything.

We know you must have something!

I'm normal. I'm as sane as you can get. I inherited his nose, nothing else. Except his feet. And hair. That's it. Oh, and his poor blood circulation, love of spicy food and highly sensitive skin. But nothing else.

C'mon, now. Take the quiz!

No! I don't need a quiz. I'm perfectly healthy.

Really? Then what are all these voices in your head? We KNOW you must have something!

So I log into Facebook. *Why should you take this quiz?* it says. *Because it's fun!* it says. Fine. I can do fun. I *know* it's just a stupid quiz that doesn't mean anything – in fact I'm proving to myself how little it means by taking it. If I had anything to hide, I wouldn't be able to do that, right?

What if you don't like the answer you get? it says. *You can just take the quiz again!* it says. Perfect. Just like real life.

I answer all ten questions really quickly and think to myself that the application doesn't give you any chance to come out as 'sane'.

How would your friends describe you?

(a) Obsessive?
(b) Paranoid?
(c) In a world of your own?

There is no *(d) Very well-adjusted to reality and an all-round top mate.* Then I click *Find out your disorder!* and it asks me to select twenty of my friends to send the application to before I can see my results. No way. So I shut the whole thing down and switch off the monitor and turn up the music and flop onto my bed.

I feel ashamed for even thinking about doing the quiz. It's not fun, it's wrong. They wouldn't make a *What Cancer Are You?* quiz, would they? With a cutesy: *C'mon, we know you're gonna get it!* But somehow it's OK to make fun of mental illness. It's OK to forget that people suffer from it and that their friends and family suffer.

Now I'm fired up and on my feet. I log in again and click *Block This Application*, shut the computer down again and start picking up clothes and tidying away CDs, because the room feels small and cluttered all of a sudden.

When it's tidy I lie on the floor and listen to the pigeons. I'm calm again. It's nice just being quiet and alone; I reckon I could stay up here for an entire week. I've got enough dirt on Raff to blackmail him for more supplies. In fact, if I just barricaded myself in here, maybe I could even survive until after the *X Factor* audition. I could probably pull the wardrobe down on its side if I emptied it first, which would go right across the door, and then the shelves could go on top of that, and that cello is pretty heavy – might as well be used for something, since I can't get a note out of it that doesn't sound like a groaning zombie.

I turn onto my front – facing the door – to build up a mental picture of the barricade: wardrobe, drawers, cello, filled suitcase – no, the cello should go on top of the filled suitcase . . . wardrobe, drawers, filled suitcase, cello. Perfect!

Oh.

My blood literally runs cold – I thought that was just an expression, but it turns out it can actually happen when you're visited by The Ghost Of Christmas Past . . .

. . . It was 17th December. I remember because before I went downstairs for breakfast I turned the date in my school diary into a rubbish doodle of a stick-girl holding a cocktail glass, and wrote: *Xmas shopping with I & C!* in the a.m. section and *C's B'day Party! (buy new mascara)* in the p.m. section.

Around the kitchen table, I didn't notice until afterwards that Mum was quieter than usual, but that's because Mum's normal level is so quiet anyway that it's like telling the difference between a whiff and a waft. Raff had taken the last of the peanut butter, but I decided that was for the best because I wanted to look thin for the party. The three of us were eating toast, and I think I was talking about whether Char's mega-strict dad would be making us play Pass the Parcel at her party.

Then we all stopped.

Dad stood in the doorway. The famous Grey Tracksuit was saggy at the knees and almost the same colour as his face. He held the butt of a cigarette, and looked at Raff and me as if we were strangers.

'Tea?' Mum said. He nodded and left, and then there was the sound of the television coming on. Mum got up and kissed the top of my head and squeezed my shoulders, and I thought: is that her way of telling me this GTD is not my fault? And if it even occurred to her to reassure me, doesn't that mean it really *is* my fault?

I looked at Raff to see if he thought so too. But he got up and put on his jacket, said something about meeting a friend and headed for the door.

'WAIT!' Dad boomed. Mum and I rushed into the sitting room. Dad was pointing the remote control at Raff, whose hand was frozen on the latch.

'What is it?' said Raff, trying to look cool though I could see the boom had gone straight through him like it had us.

'Nobody leaves.' Dad turned the television up, and flicked the channels like he always did when he was in this mood – sometimes he'll let us watch almost an entire programme and then switch it over before the last ten minutes.

'What do you mean, Paul?' said Mum. She handed him his tea. He drinks it non-stop when he's like that. Smokes non-stop, too. Eats nothing, except the odd yoghurt or a bowl of cereal. Sleeps in the day.

'I mean what I say. Nobody leaves. Look, please

don't make this difficult. I've had a terrible night and I just need to sit here and think a while.' He scratched the right-hand side of his temple with the remote control, and then put it down and lit another cigarette.

'But Dad, I'm supposed to be meeting Izzy and Char. We're doing our Christmas shopping,' I said.

'Not today.' He didn't look at me, just flicked the channels and smoked and slurped tea.

Raff went upstairs in his jacket without saying a word. I knew he was going out of his bedroom window, and I knew I couldn't do the same, and that made me angrier than ever.

'Mum, it's Char's party tonight. You have to do something.'

She ushered me past Dad and up the stairs, whispering, 'Sshh, it's OK. Don't upset yourself now. Just go upstairs and keep out of his way for today and we'll work something out.'

'What do you mean?' I whispered back.

'Sshh, trust me. I'll be up in a minute.'

I can remember feeling a tiny bit excited by the look on her face and by the fact that she wasn't just admitting defeat. I felt proud of her, and tingly inside because maybe it would be me and Mum fighting the GTD together, not letting it get the better of us.

She came into my bedroom about half an hour later.

'He's OK. He's having a nap,' she said.

'What's going on? Why doesn't he want us to go out?'

'He was up all night watching the news. Some poor

man was stabbed on his doorstep. It was a family man – he'd only gone out to ask a group of lads to turn their music down. Tragic.'

I didn't say anything for a while. Mum was staring at the floor as if she was still thinking about it, and I didn't want to interrupt or seem callous. Then she snapped out of it and gave my room a look that made me feel bad for being such a slob, which seemed a bit irrelevant at a time like this.

'Well, yes, that *is* tragic. But how does it affect me going shopping?' I said.

'It won't be for ever. You know how sensitive he is. He just wants to protect us all and sometimes it weighs very heavily on him. Be a bit understanding, Kass.'

'What, understanding about being a prisoner? We don't even live in a rough area. It's stupid – we can't live like that, we'd never go out . . . and what about the party? I'm not missing that.'

'It's fine. I'll take you to the party. Leave it to me. Just . . . just try not to upset your dad today.' As Mum left she was still giving my room the *Tidy It* look, but my mind was juggling two completely separate thoughts:

1. Is my dad right? Should we all be scared? Is the world a terrifying place?

2. I'm going to the party.

For the rest of the day, Mum and I tiptoed around Dad. We told him Raff was upstairs playing Wii. Izzy and Char didn't question my texts about having to visit relatives instead of go shopping with them, and I knew

I could make up whatever I liked later as long as I said it was Dad's side of the family, because we didn't know anything about them anyway so it seemed like one healthy step away from lying, somehow. More like 'imagining'.

I took ages in the bath, planning my outfit and wondering if I should take the miniature bottles of Baileys I knew were stashed in the laundry room (Dad was supposed to be selling them as stocking fillers in the run-up to Christmas).

I was almost ready when Mum knocked on my door. When I opened it she held her finger to her lips and motioned for me to follow. We crept down the stairs, past their bedroom door, which was ajar and revealed a duvet-covered lump: Dad. While Mum got the car keys, I grabbed three miniature bottles and stuffed them in my pocket. We went out the back.

The rush was amazing as we clicked our seat belts and set off for Char's. My calf muscles were twitching and my heart was racing and I flipped down the sun visor to check my lipstick in the mirror, flipped it up again, smiling at Mum and trying really hard not to think about Dad waking up and finding us gone.

I don't remember much about the party, except that we didn't drink the Baileys because when we opened the bottles we found mould on the rim. I know that Mum stayed downstairs in the kitchen being bored to death by Char's ultra-dull dad, while fifteen girls and Char's two boy cousins (aged twelve and fourteen, the only Y chromosomes allowed past the threshold) crammed into her room.

The rest is a blur – I think I have a bizarre form of amnesia where I forget all the fun times and remember the traumatic ones.

When Mum tried the back door on our return, it was locked. She kept pressing down the handle and pushing the door, over and over, gently, but getting more anxious each time. We stood there for a while: me looking at her, her looking at the door handle.

'Maybe Raff locked it,' she said. At that moment her phone beeped with a text message, and suddenly she started knocking loudly on the glass door.

'PAUL! PAUL!'

'Mum, what is it?' I said. Her face was taut, and she kept knocking and calling out for Dad to open up.

'You run round the front, ring the bell,' she said. But as I was leaving the back door opened.

'Quickly, quick quick!' said Dad, with his arm stretched out to herd us in, and sweat dripping from his brow as he scoured the garden path over our heads.

Inside, the house was unrecognisable. Raff was on the stairs, half-concealed in shadow. The sitting room was empty except for Dad's armchair and the television, which was on the floor. Every bit of furniture – sofas, coffee table, bookcase, television cabinet, coat rack, kitchen table, chairs – was piled up by the front door.

Dad was out of breath, and came to stand between us and the barricade. He'd lit a cigarette.

'We've got to get this door changed,' he said. 'This door is not safe.'

'Paul, what have you . . .? Right, let's just calm down for a second,' said Mum, pacing the empty space where our furniture had been.

'Me calm down?' said Dad. 'You sneak out of the house with our young daughter and take her God knows where and I'm supposed to calm down?' He took Mum by the shoulders. '*Anything could have happened!*'

She turned her face from him and I rushed over.

'Stop it, Dad, you're scaring me.'

He looked at me as if he'd only just noticed I was in the room, and let Mum go. His face changed, seemed to soften from anger but then crumple into worry.

'Are you OK?' he said.

'What have you done, Dad?'

'It's OK, it's all right,' said Mum, and she urged me over to the staircase. 'I'll deal with this. Go to bed, you two.' Raff had already disappeared.

'No, I want to stay,' I said, but I felt such a lump in my throat that I knew I didn't want to at all – most of me wanted to run and hide, but it was like passing by an accident on the motorway, and your brain telling you not to look but your body unable to turn away.

'Let her stay,' said Dad. His face changed again; the worry smoothed off. 'I haven't seen her all day. Come on, the three of us. I'll make tea.'

He went into the kitchen.

'What's happening?' I whispered.

'Um . . . he's just a bit upset. Don't worry.'

'*Don't worry?* Look at this place.'

She was; she was looking and nodding, but she

wasn't giving anything away. Then Dad came back in clutching mugs of tea – two in one hand, one in the other – concentrating hard because they were full to the brim. We were still over by the stairs. He handed the single mug to Mum, then handed one of the others to me. He took a sip and smiled at me.

'Cheers,' he said. I said it back, with the barricade in the corner of my eye. I will never forget the look on his face when he turned back to face the room.

'Grace?' he said. His mug was shaking; Mum took it off him. 'Grace, what's happened?' He ran over to the barricade as if he'd never seen it before. Then he knelt in front of it, and his head fell to his chest and his body started to shake: he was crying.

Mum motioned for me to go upstairs, and I did, to the sound of my dad snivelling in front of his crazy paranoid barricade.

That night I shut it all out. I lay in the dark, in a ball, pressing the heels of my hands into my eye sockets until I saw coloured spots and patterns, over and over until I finally fell asleep. The next day, the room was back to normal. Dad was in the armchair, smoking. He had a piece of paper by his side, and I looked over his shoulder as I passed by on my way to the kitchen: *Carbon Steel Armoured Door With Patented Locking System.*

I decide to give my bedroom a complete makeover, and play my music loud to drown out my thoughts. It's all OK, really: tomorrow is Monday, so I get to blow all this build-up of family stuff out of my head and talk about ordinary things again. Plus Christmas is over – it was ages ago – and we still have a perfectly normal front door.

Chapter Five

How To Poke A Finger In Your Best Friend's Bubble

We have a Monday morning routine on the number eighty-six. Traditionally, it has three stages – but only for me because I'm the first to get on the bus.

First stage: Kass's Virtually Aimless Brain Zigzag. This morning I'm thinking about how I always get lumbered with a part I *didn't* audition for, like when I had to be the donkey in a play at primary school, or how I got the role of The Apple Of His Eye in Dad's cringey show a.k.a. My Life, or why I'm the one out of me, Izzy and Char who cracks the silly jokes that I seem to find funnier than they ever do.

Time's up! Izzy's stop.

Second stage: Izzy's Latest Therapy-Based Observation.

'I've realised something,' she says. I'd be more

shocked if she *hadn't* realised something, because she's been theorising since the days when we still wore vests. (Wow, remember vests? Simpler days.) Izzy sits on the seat in front, sideways, and puts her bag next to her. 'OK, here it is: opposites *attract*, but they don't *last*.'

'Right.'

'It's true. You see, my dad was attracted to the way my mum is really open about emotions and stuff, and my mum was attracted to the way my dad doesn't spill his emotions all over the place, as in, he let her concentrate on her own. But in the end, he drowned in hers and she sort of died of thirst waiting for his. See?'

'Makes sense, Izz.' It is always best to agree. Izzy sits back, satisfied, as if she's just found the chemical formula for instant spot remover. And something occurs to *me* for a change. 'So, you're saying that *ideally* we need someone who is the same as us.' I'm trying not to smirk as I think about The Other Cass – OK, it's only the same name, but then how much of a sign can it be to get butterflies over someone with the same name? It's got to mean *something*.

'Not the same, exactly. It's complicated.' It always is with Izz. 'Anyway, how are you feeling?' She has that phrase down pat now. The way she says it makes you instantly remember the horrible thing you were trying your best to forget. That's the Therapist Factor.

'Kind of . . . dunno.'

'Mmm.' That *Mmm* is straight out of a psychotherapy textbook, too. It means: *carry on*.

'My dad is really into it. It's like someone replaced

him with a puppy who just discovered loo roll.'

'Mm. Can't you just be sick on the day?'

'I'd have to be in a coma. Anyway, the run-up to it is almost the same torture. It's hopeless.'

'It can't be. You've just got to make your dad realise that he can't live out his dreams through you; it's not fair.'

'I know, Doctor Freud, but how do I do that exactly?' Izzy love-hates it when I call her that.

'You just have to stay calm and explain your feelings.'

'Don't you think I've tried that?' I say, already not very calm, thanks. 'You don't know my dad.'

'But Kass, you're fifteen. He can't *make* you.'

I almost wish I hadn't told her now. She'll start waving leaflets at me in a moment.

Third stage: Char's Latest Two-Second Conversation With The Boy of Her Dreams. For nearly four years, Char has had a crush on an older boy who lives next door. This is about the only information we have on him, because Char is so superstitious she thinks that telling us any of his stats will jinx their 'relationship'. She's been impressively cunning about keeping him out of our sight. The crush might well have bordered on stalking were it not for the fact that she has the strictest dad in the world, who grounds her at every opportunity. *Bad marks? You're grounded, Charlotte. Home late? Grounded. Talking back? Grounded. Single strand of hair out of place? Grounded!!*

Dream Boy does sound lovely, in a very vague sort of way, but as Char is so nice about everyone it's really hard to tell. Izzy always says that I'm so intolerant it makes it even more special when I really like someone. Isn't that what they call a backhanded compliment?

Char sits one seat in front of Izzy, sideways like her. She is obviously bursting to tell us something.

'Guess what?'

'He proposed,' I say.

'He's gay,' says Izzy.

'No, and no,' says Char. She's much too level-headed to rise to the usual bait, but it's another tradition.

'OK, we give up, tell us what happened,' I say.

'OK!' Char is already at the clapping-squealing-seal stage and she hasn't even begun – this may indicate a conversation consisting of more than 'Hi' after only four years! Bless her. At least it's got her out of that weird mood she was in last week.

'So I just happened to be coming out of my house as he was coming along with his brother, and he said "Hi," and I said "Hi," and then he stopped right in front of my gate and said, "Hey, you go to St Agatha's, don't you?" and I said, "Yeah, why?" and he said, "Nothing, just wondering. Anyway, see you."' She is smiling so broadly it looks as if her jawbone might split. I fear for her health if he ever actually asks her out.

'Why did he want to know, do you think?' says Izzy.

'I don't know!' squeals Char. It's clear that a million possibilities have already passed through her mind, and not all of them rational.

'I guess he just wanted something more to say than

"Hi,"' I say. 'There was this boy at my house yesterday who—'

'Oh-oh-oh, wait, that's not all,' says Char. 'His brother gave me this *really* weird look as they were going inside. Kind of pervy but strange. And I was like, "Yeah right, Lucas, *as if*, you're thirteen for god's sake, get over it." And it's like, why won't his brother look at me like that?'

'Hey, that's weird,' I say. 'Raff has a friend like that. Actually, *he's* called Lucas.'

They both smile at me for this irrelevant detail. Very polite, my friends.

'So what's the next step with Dream Boy?' says Izzy.

'Ooh, I don't know. Do you think he notices that I'm always coming out of my house when he's passing?'

'Nah, he's a boy, they're thick,' I say.

'*He's* not, he goes to Dudley College, that's really hard to get into.' Char looks at me as if I've just nicked her lunch money.

'I didn't mean *he* was thick, Char,' I say. 'I just mean I doubt he's noticed because I'm sure you're very subtle, that's all.'

The relief puts colour in her cheeks again just as it's draining out of mine.

'Hang on, Char, did you say Dudley College?'

'Yeah, why?'

I don't know why I didn't think of it before, or why I'm staring the obvious in the face and having such trouble spitting it out. It's no big deal.

'Char, his name isn't Cass, is it?'

'Yes, so? How do *you* know?'

'I don't believe it.'

'*What?*'

'It can't be.'

'*What* can't it be?'

Izzy sits more upright, possibly to get away from Char who appears to be about to climb over the seat and shake it out of me.

'Umm, he was at my house yesterday, Char.' It shouldn't be such a big deal. But I have this awful feeling it's going to be.

'Don't be stupid.'

'Hey, I'm not stupid, get lost!'

'Come on, you two, no arguing,' says Izzy. 'What do you mean, Kass?'

Char has such a strange look on her face I feel like saying I made it up and just dealing with being thought of as a wind-up merchant instead of whatever it is she thinks I am. But my eyelid has started to twitch the way it does when I feel really guilty about something. I'll have to tell her.

'OK. Yesterday, Raff had a friend over. Pervy Lucas. Pervy Lucas has a big brother, and he came to fetch him. He said his name was Cass, and that he went to Dudley College, and he asked me if I went to St Agatha's and I said I did and he seemed really nice and my dad made a total arse of himself in front of him and of course brought me down with him and in the end I had to escape upstairs and he probably thinks I'm really rude or something.' It's quite a long sentence for one breath, but I had to let it all out quickly.

They are both completely silent.

'You've gone red,' says Izzy, quietly.

'I haven't.'

'You have,' says Char, not quietly, and not like Char. Suddenly I feel ultra-defensive.

'It's not *my* fault if he came to my house.'

Char shrugs. Her eyes look shiny.

'Anyway, Char, he asked you what school you go to. That means he's interested in you, he wants to know things about you. That's a sign.' I know I sound as unsure as she looks.

'He asked you too, you said.'

'That doesn't mean *anything*,' I say. 'You should have seen how rough I was looking. I wasn't even dressed. I looked like a right minger.'

Char turns round in her seat and puts her bag on her lap. This has never happened before. I reach forward and tug the shoulder of her blazer.

'Hey, Char, don't be like that.'

'Yeah, come on, Char,' says Izzy. 'Let's talk about this.'

'Char, you're being ridiculous.'

'Char, please.'

'Char, I haven't even *done* anything.'

But by now we can tell that she's crying. Half of me thinks: ARE YOU KIDDING? But the other half has that sinking feeling you get when you feel the crunch of ladybird beneath shoe. Izzy and I shrug at each other, and she mouths: *There must be more to it,* which I get after the third try. If there is, it's still with her now, as she gets up without looking at us, and goes downstairs way before we've reached our stop.

I'm not the type to stop eating in a crisis. Stress makes me more hungry. Still, these canteen chips are agony to get down. Every one sticks in my throat, and I wonder why I couldn't have been more elegant and restrained and opted for healthy tuna salad like Izzy. That would be why *she's* willowy, I suppose. That and genes.

St Agatha's chips are hardly worth having, anyway. They're not fat and hot and greasy like chip-shop chips, and served on cold plastic plates they taste like chips with their very souls sucked out. Then again, how comforting is limp lettuce? And I do feel like being comforted. Char has barely spoken to me since the bus journey. She chose the pasta with tomato sauce; I'm trying to decide what that means.

Every so often I catch Izzy and Char giving each other gentle smiles. I know Izzy's smile is designed to comfort Char rather than alienate me, but it dents my confidence every time I see it pass between them. This isn't the first time The Three Of Us has become Two Plus One, but I think it's the first time I've felt like the One. I suppose it had to be my turn sooner or later, but this doesn't feel like a good enough reason. She's being totally irrational – so why do I feel so guilty?

'Chip?' I say to Char.

'I've got pasta.'

'I know. Just thought you'd like one.'

'No thanks.'

'OK.'

I know not to offer one to Izzy. She'd wrinkle her nose and look at me as if I was voluntarily ingesting dog poo, and this lunch is unappetising enough already.

'Anyone want another water?' I say. St Agatha's girls can't be trusted with water jugs on the tables. Instead we are given thimble-sized plastic beakers and have to journey to the back of the room to fill up. We're only supposed to take two beakers to fill at a time. It's touching how much they trust us to perform orangutan-level tasks.

Izzy raises her empty beaker and nods with a mouthful of tuna. Char doesn't even look up.

'Char? What about you?'

'You've got Izzy's. You can only take two.' She starts stabbing the fusilli, unnecessarily hard, it seems to me.

'I can take Izzy's and yours. I don't mind.'

'I'll get my own. Wouldn't want to deprive you.'

'Char, I'm just trying to offer you a drink, would you just chill?'

She stops stabbing the fusilli and her eyes fill up again. I slump back down in my seat.

'Char, *please*, what is it?' She snatches her arm away from my grip. This is insane. Izzy flicks her head towards the water jug table, so I take my beaker and hers and leave.

While I'm filling them I can see Char wipe her eyes and nod and smile at Izz. Then they both get up and make their way to the exit. Izzy turns back and gives me a cute wave and a thumbs-up as they disappear to the cloakroom, where secret conversations tend to take place amongst the heavy navy coats. I down both drinks and head for the library, where people with no one else to hang out with at lunchtime tend to go.

I get to the art room first and start to prepare our table. Monday afternoons are always fun because the three of us get to sit together instead of in Two Plus One formation like all the other lessons. We sit around tables facing each other as if we're in a café, instead of in forward-facing rows of double desks like we do in every other class. It's so much more civilised (i.e. nothing like school).

As I'm choosing the best brushes and paints, sharpening pencils with the knife the way we've been shown, and hitching up the desk-top easels, I feel like I'm making up for something awful I've done. I couldn't have known that The Other Cass was Dream Boy, could I? I try to think back . . . I *couldn't* have known. Raff and Lucas have only just become mates, and Char has guarded Cass's identity with the stubbornness of a chocoholic with her last Malteser. And anyway, our meeting was a total disaster thanks to my fidgeting, my dirty face and my dad's ability to thwart every potential romance that comes my way. Not that someone like The Other Cass would ever be interested in me, so it's not really fair to blame Dad (but it helps).

Char doesn't usually do drama. She's the leveller, the voice of reason; she's the kind of nice that makes you feel permanently sinful, but in a way that makes you want to hang out with her anyway. I feel pretty mature that I'm trying so hard to be sweet to Char even though it's her who's being unreasonable. I suppose she must really, really like him. I expect a therapy session with Izzy has sorted it out – Char has always been more open to Izzy's talks than me.

Ms Wallace has already started the lesson when Izzy and Char arrive, arm in arm. Izzy looks taller, and Char's eyes are red-rimmed.

'Sorry, Ms Wallace, we had to stop off at the nurse.'

'Fine. Take a seat.' Ms Wallace is one of the more human(e) teachers at St Agatha's. Maybe it's the art Factor – she dresses in flouncy boho clothes and has cropped hair dyed peroxide blonde, and you can tell she used to wear a nose ring – because it's not as if art is about getting things wrong or right. In my experience, you either suck at it or you don't, and no amount of strictness is going to change that. She seems to have realised this, too. I'm just on the right side of not sucking. *Just.*

'Right everyone, today we're doing portraits of each other, but I want you to follow the principles of the Surrealist movement that we discussed last week.' She means putting an ear where the nose should be. No problem, I'm already feeling chaotic.

'There are reference books here at the front if anyone needs a refresher. You can talk as long as the levels don't start to interrupt my magazine reading.' She's kidding. 'I'm kidding. I'll be round to discuss your work with you. OK, get started.'

The room slowly rouses itself with the scraping of chairs and hushed conflabs about who's going to draw whom. It's easy for most because the culture at St Agatha's is a bit like Noah's Ark. Izzy and Char and I have always prided ourselves on being able to exist in a successful threesome with none of the usual bitching or piggy-in-the-middle syndrome. Syndrome! Sounds like an Izzy word. I guess it's inevitable that our little ways rub off on each other, though I don't seem to have inherited her willowyness or Char's (usually) half-full instead of half-empty view of the world. Pity.

'So, how shall we do this?' I say. I've decided to go for the Let's Forget Our Troubles And Have Fun approach, and hope I'm not overdoing it with the cheesy grin and cheery voice.

'It's up to you,' shrugs Char. She doodles a spiral in the corner of her pad.

'Well, not really. It's up to all of us,' I say. She shrugs again. 'Izz, who do *you* want to draw?'

'I think the fairest way is if I draw Char, Char draws you, and you draw me.'

I wonder if my efforts to figure out if that really is a fair way are noticeable on my face – sometimes things that come easily to some people take me a while to get. (You see now why Mensa might not have been beating my door down?) Izzy's the best at art, so at least if she draws Char, Char will get to see a brilliant picture at the end – and who doesn't like to see a brilliant picture of themselves? I only hope that Izzy's art skills can somehow get past the weirdness of surrealism so that Char comes out looking pretty even if she has wonky eyes and a building coming out of her head. Or whatever. (Maybe I should check out those reference books before I start.)

'Sounds good,' I say. 'Char?'

Shrug

That girl's going to get RSI if she shrugs any more. My patience is rapidly eroding – must . . . fight . . . it! Must . . . stay . . . NICE!

'Let's do that, then,' says Izzy. She rubs Char's arm as if she's worried our newly quiet friend might be cold. I just know it would be a bad idea for me to do the same.

For the first time ever, we draw in silence. We might as well be in maths. Smiles don't make it full circle: Izzy smiles while she's drawing Char; Char's face is like stone when she looks at me, though she giggles self-consciously when Izzy is really staring at her; I stop trying to smile at Char and instead smile at Izzy but my eyebrows are trying to form questions, like *What the hell is going on? What did Char say to you in the Secret World of Heavy Navy Coats? Why do I feel like the worst person on earth when all I did was answer my front door to a boy in brown boots?* All that just with eyebrows; I know Izzy understands every twitch, but all her eyebrows are saying back to me is *Be Patient*.

Ms Wallace is doing her rounds. We're next. I should be able to tell by her facial expression whether Char has drawn me as a Snaggle-Toothed Acne-Covered Wildebeest. She stands behind Izzy first.

'That's very touching, Isobel, you've captured the melancholy in Charlotte, well done. I like your lines. Very self-assured. Try to go just a little harder around the eyes; I think you'll like the effect. Nice work.'

Great, so Izzy is capturing some sadness in Char that I apparently put there! Now we'll have a permanent reminder of it. Ms Wallace stands behind Char.

'This is interesting,' she says, checking out Char's portrait of me. Interesting, or hideous? I need more to go on than that, Ms Wallace. There's a Best Friend Crisis playing itself out here! Ms Wallace looks at me, and then at the portrait. Me. Portrait. Me. Portrait. *What is it, Ms Wallace?*

Then I catch Izzy bending slightly to see what Char has drawn.

'Carry on,' Ms Wallace says to Char, with a squeeze of her shoulder. I shiver at the thought of mass conspiracy.

'Can I see?' I say. Without looking up, Char says:

'Nope. Not finished.'

'I don't mind.'

Char shakes her head and sniffs, takes a used tissue out of her sleeve and dabs her eyes. She's like a tap today! Fine, I don't want to see it anyway; she's probably given me two heads.

Now Ms Wallace is behind me.

'What pencil are you using?' she says.

'Umm . . . 2H.'

'It's wishy-washy, Kass. Try something darker and softer. You're not getting any depth. Maybe have another look at the books on my desk for inspiration, OK?'

Ms Wallace leaves the ten-inch knife sticking out of my back as she continues her tour of the room. Izzy gives me a look I interpret as *Poor you, but you should have used the darker pencil, you know.* I look at my portrait, which apparently has no depth and no inspiration. She's right. I have just slipped over onto the wrong side of sucking. I'm a Snaggle-Toothed Acne-Covered Wildebeest who can't draw and makes her friends miserable. And it's only Monday.

Chapter Six

The Curious Incident of the Mystery IM'er

I can tell what kind of day Mum's had by what she makes us for dinner. Tonight it's pasta with stir-in carbonara sauce, as in the kind you don't even have to heat up (but should, because otherwise the pasta is cold in seconds flat, and who wants to eat tepid pasta in a congealed cream sauce?). This dish spells stress.

Right at the top of the Good Day scale we have The Roast. A roast dinner on a weeknight means that Mum's boss spent the day in meetings away from the office rather than annoying her. (She's a PA to a man who Dad says must have grown up with the kind of fussing nanny who was still wiping the corners of his mouth when he was in his teens. Now that's Mum's job.)

Further down we have Grilled Salmon with New

Potatoes and Mangetout, which means he only asked her to do five impossible things, four of which she was able to complete (the fifth was probably 'Get me a double-thick dolphin milkshake from the planet Jupiter').

One up from the bottom of the heap is this Slightly Insipid Spaghetti Carbonara, which means he ran Mum ragged from 8.30 a.m. till 7 p.m. and then gave her a list of impossible things to be finished by tomorrow, just as he was leaving to enjoy a slap-up meal some-where swanky with the latest bimbette he's picked up. He's creepy-ancient and Dad says he dates girls who are only a few years older than me.

But at least he hasn't fired Mum again. About once a month Mum gets fired for anything from looking at him the wrong way, to wearing a jacket he finds annoy-ing, to putting too much milk in his coffee – and that means Weeknight Takeaway. Raff and I try not to revel in this monthly occasion, but as Mum always gets her job back the next day it seems wrong not to enjoy a nice Lamb Rogan Josh with poppadoms and samosas.

'Got much work to do tonight then, Mum?' I say. She's been fiddling with her hair, and jolts suddenly when she realises I'm talking to her.

'Umm, what? Oh, yes, quite a bit.' Must have been a heavy one – she's all jittery and keeps clearing her throat, and that must be her high heel I can hear tap-ping, because Dad is in his study smoking his brains out (though not in his tracksuit) and Raff is wearing those stupid giant Rudolf the Red-Nosed Reindeer slippers Mum bought him for Christmas last year. His BlackBerry is on the table and he's typing while he swizzles pasta around his fork, and almost makes his mouth every time. And I thought boys couldn't multi-task.

'Actually, I'll probably have to go out for a bit,' says Mum.

'Why, what's he got you doing now?'

'Ugh, don't ask.' She looks really on edge.

Damn, now I'll be alone and defenceless. I had a nano-chance of getting out of whatever Dad's cooking up for me in the study by persuading Mum to have a girly night of pampering – she'd straighten my hair, I'd paint her toes – because Dad avoids girly things like the plague. (He probably thinks we talk about boobs and periods, which is ridiculous because Mum is the kind of Lady who doesn't really get into conversations like that, as opposed to Izzy's mum who wants you to tell her *evvverythiiing*.)

Raff leaves the room without a word. He's probably busy transferring funds to his offshore account, and anyway no one would believe me if I said I wanted to spend the evening doing something with him – least of all him.

Mum gets up and scrapes almost an entire plate of spaghetti into the bin. If I was that stressed I'd have eaten double, followed by cake, followed by more cake, with cream. Sometimes I wonder if Mum and I are really related. Maybe they gave her the wrong baby in the hospital. Only I do have Dad's irritatingly curly hair, and although Dad manages to take over almost everything in this house I really doubt he was the one who did the giving birth part. He hollers over a paper cut.

When the doorbell rings Mum drops her plate.

'Oh! The door!' she says. She freezes and just stares at the door in terror, as if she's been on the run from the law and her time is finally up. Like my mum could even steal a free mint from a restaurant.

'Chill out, Mum, I'll get it.'

I open the door to approximately fifty red roses (I know they come in multiples of twelve, but this is no time for maths) and a small voice behind them, saying:

'For the lady of the house.'

For the first time in my life I want to be The Lady. 'Let me be The Lady!' I want to scream. 'I'm The Lady! Me! Right here! All ladylike!' Almost all of my body tries not to want the card to be signed *The Other Cass*. Kiss kiss. Etcetera.

'Mum, they're for you,' I say, with all the joy of a girl who's never even been kissed properly, except for once in a game of Sardines with creepy David who always had a cold sore. And one time with Izzy when we were ten. 'They're from . . . Mr Sizzle. Um, who the hell's he?'

'Me, of course! Who else?' In bounds Dad, like a spring lamb who's been mainlining Red Bull. He grabs Mum and kisses her as she makes these really strange yelping noises, which sound more like crying than happiness. This whole scene is doing nothing for the Parents Are Not So Weird Campaign.

Mum puts the roses in vases, until the vases run out

and she has to use the coffee pot, a spaghetti jar and a rinsed-out juice carton. She just keeps saying, 'I can't believe you did this.' Dad is singing some old song they used to dance to, apparently. Now I know where I get my unique talent from.

Poor Dad looks a bit forlorn as Mum gathers her things and heads out the door, practically bent over double apologising for having to work tonight. How can she leave when he's been so romantic? I don't know, but I'm thinking maybe one rose would have done. That's just not how my dad does things, though.

So then it's just him and me, and my least favourite word of the moment:

Rehearsal.

I could not hate the sound of my own voice more. My first attempt to put Dad off the whole *X Factor* idea has failed miserably – apparently he is only too willing to listen to out-of-tune performances of songs he hates for hours on end. The proud look on his face seemed oddly unconnected to the sound that came out of my mouth. He's some kind of aural masochist. Wow, that *is* a big word for me.

I must speak to someone normal before I go to sleep, so I take the phone up to my refuge.

The decision of who to call is pretty easy based on today's activities, but it beeps to voicemail.

'You've reached Doctor Barbara Franklin and Isobel Franklin. Please leave us a brief message and we'll get back to you. Take care!'

The instruction to be brief always makes me panic.

'Hi Izz, it's me . . . errr, nothing important, just fancied a chat. OK, so maybe I'll speak to you later, OK, hope you're well, and hi Mrs Franklin if that's you listening, I mean Doctor Franklin – I mean Barbara. OK, sorry for the long message, bye!'

I've surpassed myself.

After only five minutes in here the tip of my nose feels like ice – my radiator's been broken for a couple of weeks, but if I tell Dad he'll get his toolkit out and that's not something I like to encourage. Before I know it, he'll have caused some unnatural disaster that will mean I have to vacate the room for an indeterminable length of time, which will mean I have to share my personal space and oxygen supply with Raff, which would be . . . *shudder*.

I switch on my computer. Maybe it was Izzy's mum hogging the phone and I'll be able to MSN Izzy instead. It'd be handy if Char was on, too, because I come across much better on screen than in person and I might even be able to snap her out of her mood. But Char's dad has blocked just about every worthwhile computer programme and internet site. He's like some kind of High Priest, and he's been worse since Char's mum left them. Even a fifteen-year-old can tell that the way he behaves is more likely to drive people away than protect them. It's basic common sense. He's lucky that Char is so understanding . . . most of the time.

Izzy's online.

tallgirl: hi, on phone, how u?

curlygirl: who on phone to?

tallgirl: char.

curlygirl: how she?

tallgirl: ok sort of.

curlygirl: what's going on? don't you think she's over-reacting?

tallgirl: spose. she very sensitive.

curlygirl: yeah I know, she's my friend too.

tallgirl: I didn't say she wasn't.

curlygirl: I know.

It's hard to tell with MSN but I have a feeling Izzy's being frosty with me. What's the matter with me today? I'm haemorrhaging friends. Fortunately, I know what makes Izzy tick.

curlygirl: what do u think I should do izz?

tallgirl: I think u should say sorry and promise that u won't do anything with db.

curlygirl: WHAT??? say sorry for what? haven't done anything!

tallgirl: well u asked. and don't shout.

curlygirl: i just don't see what i'd be saying sorry for. tell me!!

tallgirl: she's convinced u're going to steal db from her. u sounded like u'd fallen for him just from one meeting.

curlygirl: did i??

tallgirl: yep. u went red and you were talking really quickly and it was really obvious kass.

curlygirl: well I haven't. that's so stupid. db is hers. as if I'd do that.

tallgirl: well I know that, but char is upset. hang on . . . kass I have to go, char can hear me typing.

curlygirl: fine. bye.

tallgirl: don't be cross. see u on bus. don't worry, we'll sort this.

tallgirl has gone offline.

I feel like my best friend just slammed the door in my face. It's eerie how far the computer can suck you in, and how quickly it can spit you out again. I scan the rest of my MSN list but there's no one I feel like talking to. I'm just about to quit when:

stix wants to chat. allow stix?

Do I know a stix? I try to think what the screen name could mean. Stix . . . sticks . . . stick insect . . . someone with skinny legs? Almost everyone in my class has skinny legs, except me, who has just-a-bit-bigger-than-normal ones, and Michelle, who hasn't got skinny anything. It could be a total stranger – I'm not sure I'm in the mood for new MSN friends, though as I'm doing so badly with my actual friends I suppose I might as well.

allow stix

stix: Is this working?

curlygirl: is what working?

stix: Oh hi. It is working then. I've never used this before.

curlygirl: not being rude but who are you?

stix: Guess.

curlygirl: not in mood sorry.

stix: Why, what's up?

curlygirl: i might tell you if you tell me who you are.

stix: Just have a guess.

curlygirl: Give me a clue.

stix: ask me a question.

curlygirl: this is tedious. OK, do you have skinny legs?

stix: Hope not, why?

(For the first time I contemplate that stix might be a boy. I don't know any girls who actively don't want skinny legs. It says a lot that I naturally assumed it'd be a girl – boys are thin on the ground in my humble existence, thanks to an all-girls school, a younger brother and not really having the sort of hair, face or body that makes boys buzz around me honeypot-style the way they do around some of the girls in my class. Izzy and Char and I are all pretty much even when it comes to experience. We don't have any.)

curlygirl: what docs stix stand for then?

stix: Drumsticks.

curlygirl: i don't know any drummers.

stix: Apart from mc.

curlygirl: grrr, why don't you just tell me who you are?

stix: This is more fun.

curlygirl: for you maybe.

stix: So far, so good. Ask more questions.

curlygirl: maybe I have better things to do.
stix: Probably. Like practise for your audition?

My heart stops. This has dramatically lowered the number of people stix could be. Who knows about my audition? Mum, Raff (and therefore Raff's idiotic bunch of followers, but there's no way any of them could maintain this kind of conversation and keep my interest, so that's them out), Izzy, and therefore Izzy's therapist, and Izzy's mum, maybe Char, and therefore maybe Char's dad as he listens in on all her phone calls. And *my* dad, of course. He was in a band in the seventies. *Please* tell me stix isn't . . .

curlygirl: Dad????
stix: I really doubt it. I was only three when you were born. Are you some kind of sicko? ☺

(Three plus fifteen equals eighteen. Wait, let me check: yes, definitely eighteen. But I don't know anyone who's eighteen, except for my cousin Jodie, but she lives in Sydney and her mum doesn't speak to my mum. I am developing a very intense headache.)

stix: I have to say I'm hurt.
curlygirl: why, did you poke yourself in the eye with your drumsticks?
stix: Haha. Lucas said you had a good sense of humour.

Bomb. Shell.
Penny. Drops.

curlygirl: Cassian?
stix: At last.

I have to get up from my desk and move away from the screen, as if he might be able to see my reaction. I fall awkwardly onto the futon and decide to stay there for a while.

stix: Kass? Are you still there?

I'll have to ignore him.

stix: Kass?

Maybe if I just cover my eyes . . .

stix: I guess you've gone. Maybe some other time then. See you around.

Is he still talking?

stix: Hope I didn't upset you or anything. Cheers. Bye.

Surely he's got the message by now.

stix has gone offline.

Chapter Seven

Apparently I Need A Warm-Up For National Humiliation

It seems like ages before I uncover my eyes, get up from the bed and look at the screen, but knowing me it's probably seconds. I'm ashamed of how energized I feel, and how much that makes me want to laugh like one of those creepy giggle n' shake toys. It comes out in small bursts that I manage to stifle by clapping both hands over my mouth. I stare at the words *stix has gone offline*, but not hard enough to change them. *Stop it, self!*

I sit back down at the computer and read over the transcript. It's hard not to smile about how well I come across – not too desperate at all, though obviously that was before I knew who he was. Some of his comments almost make the giggle n' shake monster come out again: *So far, so good . . . Lucas said you had a good sense of humour.* I always assumed it would feel like an insult for a boy to like me for my jokes – meaning that he thought I had a face like a bush pig – but by the feel of the absurd grin on my face I've obviously changed my mind.

It's not often I volunteer to go into Raff's room, but he has to be the key to how The Other Cass got my MSN name.

'Raff, can I come in?'

'What for?'

'Just need to ask you something.'

'Ask me from there.'

'Come on, Raff, it won't take a second.' The calm in my voice impresses me – I usually turn feral at the first hint of Raff being difficult, but being serene, like Mum always is with him, seems to have worked a treat because I hear him come towards the door. Then I hear the sound of him trying to turn a key without making a sound.

'When did you get a key cut?' I say.

'*Sssshhh*. What do you want?' He opens the door enough for me to see half his face.

'Let me in.'

'No way.'

'Let me in or I'll tell Dad you've got a key for your room.'

Bingo.

'Right, I've just been speaking to someone called stix on MSN.'

'Who?'

'Stix. As in drum. Come on, Raff. I know you gave

my MSN name to Cassian.'

'Who, Luke's brother? Why would *he* want it?'

'I don't know. Oh come off it, you gave it to him, didn't you? What did he say? Did he ask you about me?'

'You wish, Kass.' Forget Childline, what's the number I dial when I'm being emotionally battered by my thirteen-year-old brother? 'Hang on, I did give it to Lucas, though.'

'You *what*?'

'Chill out. He paid a fiver for it. I'll give you ten per cent.'

How I wish I was quick enough to work that sum out. Having all the scruples and none of the brains is a raw deal.

'I don't want your money. You can't just *sell* information about me. That's sick.'

'Everything is for sale, Kass. Get real.'

I don't know what is winding me up more: the fact that Raff is profiting from his friend's sad little crush on me, or the thought that it was Lovelorn Lucas on MSN all along, pretending to be his much more eligible brother. I need to read the transcript again.

Raff is just about to close the door when I manage to jam my foot in the gap. It hurts a lot more than it looks like it does in films.

'Ow! So you're saying Cassian has never asked about me, is that right?'

He smiles and shrugs. I have a flashback to belting him over the head with my Barbie (after he'd shaved all her hair off and drawn tattoos on her), and make my way back up to my room before I do something I'll regret.

If Monday was confusing, Tuesday is suspicious. When I wake I'm mistrustful of the time showing on my alarm clock; I feel as if I've only had a couple of hours' sleep. I get dressed and open my bedroom door, but as soon as I'm on the landing I have to go back into the room and check in the full-length mirror that I haven't forgotten anything crucial. Like trousers. (St Agatha's moved into the twenty-first century last year with the advent of trousers as an option. With legs like mine that was quite a triumph. Not to mention the whole feminist argument. Win-win!)

I smell the milk three times before pouring it on my cereal. Dad comes into the kitchen and just smiles before getting himself another coffee. He's up to something *else*. He's talked about the audition at every available opportunity since Saturday, and now he's silent. It's shark-sized fishiness, and possibly just as treacherous.

Mum kisses the side of my head as she passes by, harvesting keys, purse and jacket. She smells different. I bet her boss has ordered her to change her perfume. Or maybe she's always smelt that way and it's my olfactory nerve that's playing up (we learnt about that in biology the other day – you can tell it's recent information by the very fact that I've retained it. Give it another week and I'll be asking Olfactory Who?).

On the bus my Virtually Aimless Brain Zigzag is dizzying. It's as if I'm two people. I'm the misjudged friend, trying to figure out how she's hurt the nicest person she knows and anxious to make things good again. But then I'm a girl thinking of a boy; thinking of his boots and the way he could just about tuck his hair behind one ear, and thinking of the words on the screen that mean he might just like me too. If I could stay two people, maybe I could make the boy two people as well. Then Char could dream about her Dream Boy, and I could dream about The Other Cass. They are already different people in my head. Almost.

When Izzy gets on I realise how desperate I am to tell someone about the MSN chat last night, and about my suspicion that it may have been Lucas instead of his brother. To put it mathematically, which I wouldn't usually do only the chaos of the situation seems to be calling for something pragmatic, I'm sixty-five per cent sure it was The Other Cass. More importantly, I'm thirty-five per cent doubtful.

'Hi. How was Char last night?' I say.

Izzy shrugs, and then breathes out heavily as if she hasn't exhaled for hours. *Why* do people keep *shrugging* at me?

'Izz, I wouldn't ever *do* anything, you know. I love Char.'

'I know. Anyway, it's not as if he even fancies you, is it? It's just that Char has had a thing for him for so long. It's weird how much it's affected her.'

I'm nodding, though I feel suddenly very far away and wounded by Izzy's perfectly reasonable statement: *it's not as if he even fancies you.* I feel so silly.

'So why don't you just say sorry, swear on your life you'll never get off with him, and we can all go back to normal.'

'Fine.'

'Excellent. We're nearly at her stop. So, how's your dad? Any more weirdness? Have you talked about songs yet?'

I know Izzy's talking, I know she's expecting me to answer, but my needle's got stuck.

'Kass?'

'It's not fine, actually.'

'Oh, God, what now? Honestly, all this conflict is giving me a headache.' She pinches the bridge of her nose the way I've seen her mum do a lot.

'Is it? Because you seemed to quite enjoy it yesterday.'

'Enjoy it? What are you on about?'

I'm not sure. But now it's out I feel like I have to carry on.

'Just the way you sided with Char straight away.'

'What? I didn't side with her. She was upset.'

'*I* was upset!'

'What about?'

How weak would it sound if I said 'I don't know'? But I don't, I just know that whatever words are coming out of my mouth now feel true.

'Let's just forget it,' I say.

'You can't say that now.'

'Well, I just did.'

'God, talk about extremes.'

Ouch.

That settles it – I decide to keep myself to myself for the rest of the day. See how they like being frozen out like they're doing to me.

Before we're dismissed for the day, Mrs Roach, our form tutor, says she's got some information she's sure we'll be glad to stay behind for. Knowing her, it'll be about maths tutorials or being in the summer musical. You'd think with the amount of time teachers spend in the company of teenagers they'd have a better handle on what makes us tick.

'This Friday there will be a disco at St Joseph's.'

Pardon-sorry-what? A social, non-academic event involving St Agatha's girls and St Joseph's boys being allowed in the same room? I may even gloss over the fact that Mrs Roach said the word disco. For now.

'The event will raise money for Children in Need . . .'

Here's the bit where she ruins it by telling us we all have to wear red noses while we 'boogie'.

'. . . and the main attraction will be the karaoke machine!'

Thud. That was the sound of my head falling to my desk. Karaoke is the very last thing I need in my life.

'In fact, a very kind St Agatha's parent has agreed to organise our own version of *The X Factor*. There'll be judges and voting and a really spectacular prize for the winner. So if everyone could . . .'

Mrs Roach's voice fades into the background as a

miniature of my dad doing his Gollum impression leaps onto my desk. *It's you, isn't it, Dad? This unspeakable event has got your name all over it.* Gollum scuttles into his cave, muttering, 'The winner you will be, my precious, Gollum will fix that . . .'

This is bad.

The *X Factor* audition seemed far away, not to mention far-fetched, and totally separate from my life at school – it was just this small-but-dreadful thing I had to do for my dad, to keep what happened back in December *back in December* and not returning to haunt us. Behind closed doors.

But this 'disco' is three days away in a church hall up the road, and people I know will be there. Plus people I don't know. People! In public! And now the rest of my week will be tied up with Dad nagging me about songs and looks and self-belief and aiming high and the right food and the right outlook and potential and talent and the bloody pot of stupid gold at the end of the damn rainbow.

No wonder he was so quiet this morning; I'd feared it was the start of another GTD but he was just conserving energy to ruin my life even more.

Rapid thaw required: I need my friends right now. Lashings of sympathy like hot sweet custard from Char, and nuggets of practical advice like vitamin pills from Izzy.

'Char, Izzy – I'm sorry.' I get a smile from Izz and a one-armed shrug from Char. 'Char, he was just there for a second. I couldn't even pick him out of a row of people who don't actually look like him – that's how significant the whole thing was. I didn't like him – I mean, not that he wasn't nice, he was, just not my type – and he *definitely* didn't look twice at me. He was looking at the Wii the whole time. And anyway, Char, I would never, ever do anything to hurt you. Cassian is off limits. Friends come first.'

Suddenly Char throws herself at me and cries something into my blazer that eventually becomes audible:

'Sorry, babe. It's not you, it's . . . sorry, babe.'

Izzy gives us a triumphant therapist beam.

'Oh no, your blazer.' Char sniffles the remains of what's now smeared on my shoulder and tries to wipe me with her sleeve.

'It's fine. Don't worry.'

'Sorry for being so . . .'

'Don't worry,' I say. She looks so sweet, all tear-stained and happy again, which makes the nagging feeling I have, that this isn't at all over, feel like poison.

Chapter Eight

Why Have One Totally Weird Parent When You Can Have Two?

Both of my elbows are resting on red apples; my head rests in my hands. It's dinner time, and the suspicion that's been gnawing away at me all day has split open with Mrs Roach's earth-shattering announcement. As Izzy would say, *better out than in* (and she doesn't mean wind – as if Izzy would ever advocate farting). So now the boil is lanced, and I just need to deal with the pus. (I did say it was dinner time, didn't I? Maybe I'll forget about the pus until afterwards.)

The way Dad plonks himself down at the table next to me, all breathless and smiling as if he's just sprinted here from his Life-Wrecking Laboratory, makes me desperate to fling him a sarcastic line about Friday night, but I've already decided not to involve Mum and Raff. This time I'm going to try a calm, serious talk, just

Dad and me.

I need sustenance first.

Nobody speaks when Mum puts dinner on the table. We look at the plates, then at each other, then at the plates again, then at Mum, who is winding spaghetti carbonara around her fork.

'Another bad day, love?' says Dad.

'Sorry?'

'We had carbonara last night,' says Raff.

'Oh, did we?'

Mum carries on eating as if she hasn't for days. As for the rest of us, our forks are hovering but not yet committing.

'If you don't like it,' she says, 'just eat the salad.' She doesn't sound cross, and she isn't apologising in that *Stepford Wives* way that used to make me cringe. She's just very matter-of-fact, and clearly *very* hungry. I like it. I'm also horrified by the thought of how empty I'd be if I just ate salad, so I dig my fork in and eat with the same enthusiasm as her.

'It's nice, Mum,' I say. I think that's a smile but she doesn't look at me – she's busy piling green salad onto her plate and folding huge lettuce leaves through her wide open lips, which are now wet with salad dressing and chewing eagerly. She's fascinating.

'I'm out again tonight,' she says with her last mouthful. She clears away her plate while the rest of us are still ploughing through our meals. 'Have to do a few things for you-know-who.'

'I've got loads on anyway,' says Dad. He winks at

me; I scowl. Mum carries on as if she hasn't heard him. We chew and chew as she gathers her coat, leaves the room, comes back in with her head half in her bag, looks in the general direction of the table and swings around as she says, 'See you then.'

At the click of the front door, all's very still.

'What was all that about?' I say. Dad and Raff munch seriously, with strands of spaghetti tumbling from their lips. I take an unsubtle look underneath the table and see that Raff's right hand is typing (he's probably remortgaging the house). Dad's legs are jiggling. I wonder if they even noticed how un-Mum-like Mum seemed.

'I've got to talk to you about something,' says Dad. 'There's this little thing on Friday I've sort of organised.'

I start gulping water to wash back what I really want to say about that.

'It's nothing to get worked up about, Kassidy, but I do want you to have a little, err, *sing* at this small party I've planned. A warm-up, I suppose.'

'Dad, can we talk about this later?'

'What for? Seize the moment! Look, I've written down a few songs I think you could do. It'd be the perfect dry run – all your friends there, cheering you on.'

I'm trying really hard to stay calm, but what's the point if it's just not working?

'I've highlighted the ones I think we should practise tonight. No calls or TV, OK, Kassidy? I don't want any of your nonsense on this.'

I can feel it all bubbling inside me, carbonara about to curdle.

'We'll talk hair and wardrobe tomorrow – I want to steer you away from this grungy look you've adopted. Fresher, Kassidy! Pretty! You look so depressing sometimes.'

Right, that's it.

'I'm *not* doing it.' I smack an apple. 'I can't believe you've organised this behind my back, for a start. I can't believe you expect me to do something that makes me feel physically sick. And I don't even know why I can't believe it, because you are *always* stuffing things up for me.'

'Kassidy, please—'

'Why can't you just leave me to be ordinary?' I stand up, clutching the salad bowl and my half-full plate, walk away from Dad's horror-struck face and let the dishes clatter onto the draining board. I'm shaking and all the muscles in my back feel like they're being pulled into a central point by wire.

'You're not ordinary, Kassidy.'

'I am, to *everyone* but you. I don't see Mum jumping up and down about my many "talents", and Raff certainly doesn't think I'm anything special.'

'It's true, I don't,' says the boy with one finger up his nose.

'See, Dad? So *why* can't you just drop all of this and just let me be . . . *me*?'

He's like a chameleon. Just a second ago he looked like an overbearing bully, albeit a fairly small and scrawny one. Now he looks like a child who's just learnt that he hasn't been good enough for a visit from Father

Christmas this year. I turn around to face the sink again but it's no good, I can see him reflected in the window.

'As entertaining as this is, I've got stuff to do,' says Raff, and against the inky sky I see the tiny figure of my brother going upstairs to get on with his life in peace. Dad's been quiet a long time. I dare to hope that he might actually have heard me.

'Kassidy, this will be the last thing, I promise. I just know I'm right about you – you're *not* ordinary. I'm so, so excited about this. I haven't felt like this for . . . look! Look at my hands, I'm shaking with the buzz of this!'

Against my better judgement I turn and look. He is.

'I tell you what, Kassidy – I'll email you the songs I've been thinking of, and you can go upstairs, go through them and see which one feels right. Then come down and we'll get to work. OK? That's fair.'

He reaches across the table to my mobile phone, but his hand stops just short of picking it up, and he looks up at me with his impish grin.

'I'll leave that there.'

He pats it and leaves.

I could scream. He's like a massive lorry with no brakes, steaming around a racetrack honking its horn – it's all about this lorry, nothing else on the track matters, around and around, and I'm driving in the opposite direction, but every time we're heading for each other I swerve right out of the way. I don't want him to keep going round, but I can't let him crash.

* * *

In my room, I sit with the lights out. I'm on my bed in the dark underneath the cooing and the patter of rain, as far away from my computer as possible. In a room this size it means I can still smell it. Every muscle in my body is being used to fully resist logging onto MSN. In contrast it takes zero effort to resist reading the email Dad will have sent.

I dial half of Izzy's number. Hang up. I dial half of Char's and wait for the woman to tell me that the number I have dialled has not been recognised. *Please try again.* I know that this fight with Char felt worse because it was our first, but now I wonder if I really know her, or her me. In a million years I wouldn't have been able to predict the way she's been with me this week. And the way she was behaving, it's as if she thinks I'm some kind of Career Boyfriend Stealer. It's ridiculous – I have absolutely no powers where boys are concerned. I'm a Career Boyfriend Repellent – I think I was born with an invisible garlic bulb around my neck.

Rehearsal in Dad's study is exhausting. Maybe it really would be better to be one of those people who think they can sing when they can't. I would rather listen to anything else: nails down a blackboard, retching, someone hawking up loads of phlegm and then spitting it out, *anything*. Unfortunately the look on Dad's face is very *Hark! The Herald Angels Sing!*

I just do what I have to do to keep him quiet, and afterwards I'm too stressed out for anything but sleep.

– *Hang on, we've seen you before, haven't we? Katie Something-or-other.*

– *Kass Kennedy.*

– *Sounds like a speech impediment. Anyway, what brings you back?*

– *My dad wants me to have another go, Mr Cowell.*

– *Your dad? Oh, give me strength. I am so bored of parents plonking their talentless children in front of me and begging me to make them stars. Have you got star quality, Katie?*

– *I don't think so, no.*

– *So why don't you just tell your dad you'd rather not come here night after night wasting my time? Hmm?*

– *Well, I'm a bit worried about what he might do.*

– *Do? What, to me? Look, you know I have bodyguards. I can call them in any time; they're huge, and they can—*

– *Calm down, Mr Cowell. He's not going to touch you. He's not like that. He sort of . . . turns in on himself. He folds up, shuts down, whatever you want to call it. If I say no, it's like I'm pushing down the lid on a jack-in-the-box: he's going down and down, you can see he doesn't want to, and then he's gone, and you're left there just waiting for the next moment he'll pop up, only you're not entirely sure he will.*

– *Err, right. Very deep. You mean he's a fruit loop.*

– *No! Don't talk about him like that.*

– *OK, OK, I'm sorry. Back to business, seeing as I'm stuck with you. So, if you haven't got star quality, what other qualities have you got?*

– *Erm . . .*

— Today, preferably, darling.

— Sorry, Mr Cowell. Well, I'm a good friend.

— Really? That's not what I heard. I heard you couldn't stop thinking about Char's boyfriend, and that even now that you're fast asleep you're itching to log onto MSN to see if stix is there.

— But I didn't. I haven't. And he's not her boyfriend.

— Yes, yes — you didn't. Yet. But it's the wanting to, isn't it, Katie?

— Is it, Mr Cowell?

— 'Fraid so. Now, are you going to sing me something or not? Preferably nothing to do with fish fingers.

— How about 'Anytime You Need A Friend'?

— I don't think so.

— OK, 'You've Got A Friend In Me'?

— Absolutely not.

— I can sing the theme tune from Friends *if you like.*

— Fine, give it a whirl, whatever.

. . .

— Well, come on, then!

. . .

— Oh, marvellous — chaps, she's wet herself again. Someone get her off . . .

Chapter Nine

What Has Four Wheels, Two Eyes, And Makes My Heart Go Thumpety-Thump?

Sometimes when life accelerates you get so used to the new speed that it's a jolt when it slows down to normal. When I woke on Wednesday morning my mind was still racing, but Wednesday was covered in speed bumps: complicated maths lessons, Izzy's latest argument with her dad (about her mum, naturally), and Raff sitting next to someone at the bus stop who was eating KFC. There wasn't time for anything else.

Dad orders takeaway curry in the evening because Mum has to drive her friend Sue to a Pilates class, because Sue's husband is abroad and Sue's car has broken down. Mum goes into great detail about the husband and the trip and the mechanical problems of the Volkswagen Bora, and I can tell we all want to say,

'So what?' at some of the trivia but we don't. I suspect that was because Mum so rarely talks for that long in one go that we were pretty curious as to what was going to come out: who would have guessed it'd be Sue's oil pump?

Amazingly, Dad doesn't talk about the Unholy Mess that is Friday night's 'disco', but he doesn't have to because it's all there, simmering away under my skin. He eats like he's fuelling himself for something big. Raff takes a naan, plonks a load of chicken korma in the middle and folds it over so he can eat it one-handed. I eat slowly but steadily, almost rhythmically, like I've been programmed.

Soon the curry's gone, unless you count the onions in the sauce at the bottom of the container, or the bag of onions we're never sure what to do with, or the half-eaten onion bhaji. I wonder how many onion trees are pointlessly decimated just to end up in people's bins, until I remember that onions don't grow on trees.

Raff says: 'Dad, Lucas is coming over in a sec because we're doing a joint project.'

Was I just thinking about onions? Lucas is coming over!

'That's nice. What's the project?' says Dad.

Who cares! When's he coming, Raff? He can't be coming alone, not at thirteen years old and in the dark, can he?

'It's on the . . . Brazilian rainforest.'

Of course it is, Raff. Very convincing.

'Sounds good. Do we need to pick him up and drop him off, though, because Mum's got the car?'

Someone else is dropping him off, Raff, aren't they? *Aren't they?* Speak, boy!

'I think one of his lot is.'

Suddenly I'm thinking about onions again, only now it's the worry of whether I smell of them, and about that pallid, swollen look I get when I've just stuffed my face. On the other hand, repelling him with onions might be exactly what a true friend would do.

I clear away the takeaway rubble and find myself wiping down the apples with a J Cloth. In the sitting room I smack each cushion and throw them back on the sofa casually until they look exactly right. The newspapers go in one pile on the coffee table; the remote control goes on the arm of the sofa; I kick my clunky school shoes behind a giant plant pot.

'What are you doing?' says Raff.

'Nothing.'

'Yeah, right. Anyway, Dad wants you in his study.'

'Why should I? I'm not going to his stupid party. It's not fair; it's so embarrassing, I just can't.' It's unclear who I'm appealing to. The giant plant pot, perhaps?

'Whatever, Kass,' says my ever-supportive brother. 'But just so you know . . . oh, but I'm sure you're not interested. I'll just keep it to myself.'

'Know what? Come on.'

'Nah, you wouldn't be interested.'

At the sound of our doorbell I run up to my room two stairs at a time, nearly stumble backwards at the top and have to clutch the banister. I crouch there, trying to catch my breath but having to hold it so I can make out the voices downstairs. I can hear my dad, though not exactly what he's saying; they must still have the front door open and the sound is travelling out the wrong way. By the tone of his voice I know he's not talking to either Raff or Lucas.

The front door closes. I run into my parents' room and wrestle with the net curtains, trying to reach the window. A figure walks to a little yellow car. I've opened the window before I have any idea what to say, and it's not exactly the sort of weather for randomly opening windows.

'Hi,' I call out, and then duck back inside and contemplate stuffing my mouth with net curtain.

'Kass?'

Oh God, it is definitely him.

'Yeah, hi. I was just looking out for my friend.'

'Right, cool. I just dropped my brother off. So, how are you?' He walks closer, hands in pockets. He's wearing the brown boots again. Not for my benefit, obviously.

'Yeah, brilliant, thanks.' Brilliant? Never has a word been more uncool.

'Good, because I was worried I'd offended you the other night.' He kicks the kerb and nearly stumbles, and then kicks it again as he recovers. The goofiness is even more appealing than the boots.

'Offended me? No way. I just had to go.'

'OK. That's good, I mean.'

More kerb-kicking. I hope I'm far enough away so

that he can't hear my teeth chattering; it's so cold and I'm only in my school shirt. I hear a fox and very nearly start a conversation about the terrible screeching noise vixens make when they're ready to mate. Thank God he speaks first.

'I'm supposed to be studying but I feel like going for a drive.'

'Sounds good. I like your little car.'

Rewind. *Rewind.* He'll think you want to go for a drive with him. And should I have referred to his car as *little?*

'It's a shame you can't come along.'

I can't? Should I remember why *I can't?*

'Have a nice time with your friend, then. See you, Kass.'

Oh, that's right, I'm leaning out of this window waiting for my friend. *Stupid, stupid friend.*

'Yeah, see you, Cass.'

He walks to his little yellow car, and puts the key in the lock.

'I guess I'll see you Friday, then,' he says, getting in but leaving one long leg on the pavement.

'Pardon? Why's that?'

'I'm one of the bouncers for that party. Your dad asked me.'

GIRL ASPHYXIATES SELF WITH NET CURTAIN.

'Oh right! Great, that's . . . *great.*'

GIRL FOUND FACE DOWN IN VERY SHALLOW POOL OF ENTHUSIASM.

'He said you were going to be singing.'

'That's the plan. Dad's plan, that is. I'm not exactly very good.'

GIRL CRUSHED TO DEATH BY MASSIVE UNDERSTATEMENT.

'I bet you're being modest. I'm thinking my band might do the *X Factor* thing. Had a quick chat to your dad about it – he's a top bloke, reckons we should all just go for it. He's so positive, isn't he?'

What is my dad playing at now? Is he going to lead the entire population of teenagers down to the X Factor *auditions like the Pied Piper?*

'Um, I guess that's one word for it. He can be kind of a pain.'

'Yeah, well, what would I know? He's your dad. I haven't even seen mine since I was two.'

GIRL SMASHES SKULL AFTER TOPPLING OUT OF FIRST-FLOOR WINDOW WHILE TRYING TO RETRIEVE PREVIOUS SENTENCE.

'Oh! Sorry.'

'Not your fault.' He smiles and shrugs. 'Anyway, I thought it'd be cool knowing someone else who's doing the audition.'

GIRL RECONSIDERS SUICIDE PACT WITH SELF.

'It would, yeah . . . What are you laughing at? What's funny?'

'Sorry, nothing. You're kind of weird, Kass – nice weird, I mean.'

He thinks I'm nice? He thinks I'm weird? He thinks I'm something?

GIRL DECIDES SUICIDE DEFINITELY OUT FOR NOW.

'Thanks, I guess.' Thank God I don't say, *You're nice too*.

'You're nice too.'

No!!!! Recover! Recover!

'Um, I'd better save my voice. Night air and stuff.'

'OK, bye then, Kass. See you Friday.' Wow. There should be some sort of government health warning on his smile. Warning: may cause loss of morals.

'Friday. OK. Bye.'

Suddenly I freak out about the net curtains draped on my shoulders looking suspiciously like a bridal veil, so I shake them off and close the window as he draws his leg into the little yellow car. He's away up the street and I'm heading for my room and I have

Absolutely

No

Idea

What To Do.

Chapter Ten
Attack Of The Killer Conscience

I get through that evening's rehearsals with Dad by being somewhere else. *Ish.* My body is in Dad's office, making some pretty inhuman sounds, but my mind is outside in the street with The Other Cass. I keep going over the same imaginary scene: I open the front door and he's standing there, hands in his pockets, head to the side and a killer smile. He puts his arm around me as we walk towards his little yellow car (I seem to be draped in a net curtain). But then we stop – something's not right. Either I say something stupid or I trip over or the car turns into a giant banana. So then back I go to the front door and replay the whole thing.

'Are you OK, Kassidy?' says Dad. 'You seem . . . distracted.'

'I'm just visualising,' I say. Which is not a lie.

'Good girl. Only, try not to visualise when you're

actually performing because you get a dopey expression when you do it. OK?'

'Fine. Is this over now? I'm tired.'

'We should really do another—'

'My voice, Dad, I mean my voice is tired. It's not good to strain it, you know that.'

'Sorry, you're right – I'll fetch you a glass of salt water to take up with you.'

As I log onto MSN the last of the salt crystals sink to the bottom of the glass, but nothing about me feels settled. I almost can't look at the screen in case he's there.

He's there!

I'll pretend I haven't seen him. If I sit here and chat to someone else, or Google something – I'm sure I need to Google *something* – there's no harm done, is there?

stix: hello

It'd be rude not to say hello. Just hello and then I'll make an excuse.

curlygirl: hi
stix: nice time with your friend?
curlygirl: yes thanks
stix: what else you been doing?
curlygirl: not much
stix: you OK? Don't seem very chatty. Want me to go?

Here it is: the perfect way to get rid of him. Say

you're tired, say you have studying to do, say you're off for a bath – no, don't say bath or he might think you're trying to make him think about you naked!

curlygirl: Don't go. Sorry, I was just distracted by something but I'm OK now.

Interesting. Still, I suppose a quick chat wouldn't hurt. You could even find out some stuff about him to tell Char. Think of it as a favour to a friend.

curlygirl: did you go for a drive?
stix: quick one, popped in to see a mate.
curlygirl: someone in your band?
stix: used to be. There was a big fight about him and he got kicked out.
curlygirl: Oh. Why, wasn't he good enough? What did he play?
stix: Bass. He's a genius. But he's got ADHD and it pissed everyone off.
curlygirl: Doesn't seem very fair. Why?
stix: Complicated. He's just harder to be with, I guess, than most other people – well that's what they thought, it's not what I think.
curlygirl: Hard in what way?
stix: Lots of things that 'normal' (whatever they are) people do, only Tom does it all the time – like forgetting we had rehearsal, or interrupting people a lot, fidgeting, kind of wound up, like his motor is powered

by some amazing kind of fuel and he's not in charge. I dunno, I'm probably not explaining it very well. But he's cool. I like him a lot and I felt bad for not being able to convince the others to keep him.

curlygirl: sounds like you did your best. You can't make people understand sometimes.

Stix: You sound like you've been there.

How has it come to this? I want to tell him about Dad. Should I? Why *would* I?

stix: Sorry, was that too personal? You've gone quiet ☹

curlygirl: No, it's fine. Sorry. Was just thinking.

stix: About . . . ?

curlygirl: Just about your friend. I don't talk about this much, so swear you won't tell?

stix: I swear. On my drum sticks ☺

curlygirl: ☺ OK, well, it's about my dad. He's got a disorder, kind of like your friend. Not that, though. Something different.

I can't believe I'm telling him. It feels dangerous, but it feels right.

stix: Do you know the name of it?

curlygirl: Yep. Cyclothymic Disorder. That's what we think anyway.

stix: I haven't heard of it.

curlygirl: Have you heard of bipolar?

stix: Beethoven had that.

curlygirl: Oh, didn't know that! Isn't Britney supposed to have it?

stix: Britney and Beethoven – who knew they had so much in common??

curlygirl: ☺ Anyway, my dad doesn't have that, but it's like a mild form of it. It can turn into bipolar. That's what we worry about. A lot.

stix: how likely is that?

curlygirl: don't know. I know I must sound really stupid but I don't know much more about it.

stix: you don't sound stupid at all. Must be really hard. Is he in treatment for it?

curlygirl: No. He won't. He gets scared when he's really low – like, scared of everything – but then when he's 'up' he doesn't think there's anything wrong at all. He's in one of his 'up' cycles now, which means he's so enthusiastic he could almost levitate. That's how all this *X Factor* stuff got started.

stix: You mean you don't want to do it?

curlygirl: ☹

stix: Seems harsh. What would happen if you just said no?

This is getting too hard. I've said enough. I feel like crying.

stix: Kass? Are you still there?

stix: Your dad seems really nice. Must be difficult. Don't be upset.

curlygirl: He'll be ok. I'd better go.

stix: Really? Stay – let's talk about something else if you like. Anything: particle physics, organometallic compounds, crystallography . . .

curlygirl: I could talk at length about any of those, to be honest. Are you a geek?

stix: a tiny bit. Sshh. Swear you won't tell.

curlygirl: I swear. On your drumsticks.

stix: ☺ Are you sure your boyfriend won't mind you staying up all night talking to me?

Dilemma: do I tell The Other Cass that I've never ever ever in my fifteen long years had a sniff of a boyfriend? Or . . .

curlygirl: Actually I broke up with someone a while ago. He was a jerk. Immature. Anyway, back to particle physics.

An hour later I finally say goodnight to The Other Cass. I log out, and then print our entire conversation and shove it in my desk drawer. My eyes ache from staring at the screen so long, or maybe my treachery is turning me blind.

I lie on my bed, spread out like a starfish. My mind is whirring, so I concentrate hard to make everything get in line: first I wonder if I would have gone for a drive with him if I hadn't inadvertently turned down the invitation by mentioning the mysterious Friend. Then I wonder how I would have convinced my dad to let me. Then I wonder why on earth someone like him is asking someone like me to get into his little yellow car, or talking to me all night on MSN. Then I wonder how the hell I'm going to get through Friday night. Then I wonder why I'm even contemplating going now. *Especially* now that he's going to be there. Then I wonder what it means that I could tell The Other Cass about my dad but I don't even talk about it with my best friends. Then I think of Char.

She shouldn't be that far down the list. Char deserves better. So what if I've already had more of a conversation with him than she has managed in four years? So what if it's him flirting with me and leaving his long leg hanging out of the little yellow car door as if it's in any way possible not to like it? And who cares if he's the only guy I've felt this loopy over who's ever shown a flicker of an eyelash of interest in me?

It's like a sickness. This must be what they mean by two-faced, because I really feel like two people at the moment. There's probably some psychological term for it that Izzy could enlighten me with, only something tells me I can't trust Izzy with this new information. I have a pretty good idea which side of the fence she'd stand on. Because there is a fence, I have to admit. It's gnarled and ugly and I'll get splinters in my bum if I sit on it much longer.

I'm so far into my thoughts that I'm only just aware that my mobile has lit up.

CHAR CALLING

'Hello?'

'Hey, Kass.'

'Hey. Are you OK? You don't usually call me in the evening.'

'Oh, I'll hang up then.'

'No! I didn't mean that. I just wondered if you were OK.'

'I guess so. You?'

'Yep, I'm fine.'

This is dreadful. I can't think of a single thing to say to her.

'So what's going on at your place tonight?' she says.

'Usual. Dad's plotting my downfall. Mum's busy running errands for her boss. You know what he's like: "Get me a Triple Thick Wheatgrass Shake Squeezed By The Silken-Covered Feet of Albino Shetland Ponies." He's always on some health kick that Mum has to cater for.'

'Oh, really? So she'll be out all evening?'

'Um, yeah, although I guess she could be back now – I've been in my room.'

'Right.'

'Doing homework.'

'OK.'

'Yeah, *Death of a Salesman* essay.'

'OK. I have to go actually.'

'Err, OK. Are you all right, Char?'

'Yep. Bye, Kass.'

When she hangs up, tears sting my eyes and I have a horrible premonition about what it would feel like if that were our last ever conversation. Was it Char who was being super-weird just then or was it me? My nana always says you should never let the sun go down on an argument, but what about the day after an argument – your first argument – when things are still strained and you've just had a bizarre conversation about your mum's boss and your English homework?

I call her back.

Voicemail. Only it's Char's dad's voice, which doesn't make leaving a message any easier.

'You're through to Charlotte's voicemail. Leave a brief message with your name and number.'

'Char, it's Kass again. Bit crazy, cos I know we've only just spoken but . . . are you all right? Um, sleep well. See you tomorrow, babe.'

It's suddenly simple. It's my kind, always-there-for-me friend, who hardly ever complains (even about her Sergeant Major Dad, though Izzy and I both know what a control freak he is) and puts her friends first and hasn't had a single sniff of luck since her mum left without so much as a goodbye note versus Some Boy.

No contest. Char means far more to me. This was all just a blip – a distraction from the real problem in my life: Dad.

Chapter Eleven

Have Myself A Merry Little Christmas Pud

We're in our usual formation on the bus; Char has just joined us. Her cheeks were icy when she kissed us hello, and now she blows warm air into her cupped hands and rubs them. She hasn't smiled yet but I suspect it's just the cold. Anyway, I'm about to tell her something that will take her mind well away from the weather.

'Guess what, Char?'

'What?' She doesn't look at me, but hunches her shoulders and shivers and cups her hands again. I don't remember it being *that* cold outside.

'I know where a certain someone is going to be tonight.'

'Who?'

I just grin at her and nod.

'You mean . . .?' She gasps; I think she gets it.

'Yep. He's coming to the karaoke.'

Izzy shoots me a worried glance, not knowing that I'm about to make everything all right, and Char springs to life – the slightly hyper side of life.

'He's not. Is he? Why is he? Why would he? Oh my God. My dad even said I could go. Oh my God. Is he really?'

'Let's just calm down,' says Izzy. She takes one of Char's thin pink hands from the bus seat and rubs it between hers.

'I just found out,' I lie. 'Lucas was over to see Raff and I overheard them saying that Cassian had been asked to be a doorman.' Another lie, but for the best, I figure.

'But isn't your dad organising this thing? How come he didn't tell you?' says Izzy. Who is she, Veronica Mars?

'Dad's just organising the actual karaoke, I think. Anyway, Cassian hasn't been around again so I don't know when Dad could have asked him. So it can't have been. Dad, I mean.' Strike three. I really hope that's enough lies to cover it up so that Char can just enjoy the information rather than wondering where it came from.

'I feel sick,' she says. 'I can't go.'

'Don't be silly, Char. This is your chance,' I say.

'Really? Will you help me? I mean, come home with me after school, help me get ready, just . . . *please*, Kass, you have to *help* me.'

She looks like she's facing a leg amputation. Apparently I'm the anaesthetic.

'Wouldn't Izzy be better? She's much calmer than me, and better at make-up.' (OK, that really *is* a lie. Izzy's a natural beauty, which is lucky because she puts make-up on like Jodie Marsh in a hurry.)

'I've got therapy,' says Izzy.

'And I *need* therapy,' says Char. 'Please, Kass.'

'Umm, OK. Sure.' She doesn't notice the hesitation in my voice, but it's because I haven't brought my took-me-three-hours-to-choose outfit with me, and I usually spend some time on my own before an ordeal like karaoke – I'm better that way. I can't let her down now, though. This could be all I need to fix the weirdness between us for good.

Everyone's talking about tonight. The fact that we're getting worked up about an evening with St Jo's boys shows just how sparse social events are. All work and no play makes St Agatha's girls . . . well, *desperate*, by the sounds of it. Boys who spit at the bus stop are suddenly given Hollywood status. Boys who have been known to crumble an entire packet of crisps and empty it down your neck on the bus suddenly have 'really good bone structure' and 'nice hands'. Char just smiles. I bet I know what she's thinking; I bet it's the same thing I'm thinking. Only she's allowed to. Those boys are nothing compared to The Other Cass. It almost makes it more romantic that I'm going to help my friend get off with the boy I like. I bet there's a play by Shakespeare about this exact situation. I should read it. Or better still, watch the film so that I actually have some hope of understanding it.

On the bus journey home I start to fixate on my lack of outfit. Char sits next to me instead of in front of Izzy, who is penned in by a bald man whose leather jacket smells like Playdoh.

'Don't worry, you can wear anything of mine,' says Char.

'The skinny jeans?' I say.

'Oh.'

'I'm kidding, babe. As if I'd even fit into them.'

'You would,' she insists, very high-pitched.

'OK, I'll wear those.'

'Oh.'

'Char, I'm KIDDING!'

'Well, stop it, I have no sense of humour in a crisis!' She links arms with me. Izzy shifts around in her seat, trying not to touch Playdoh Man, and makes an *Ahhhh* face. As much as I love Izzy I wish she wouldn't think she can fix my life all the time. It's me who's put Char and me back together. And did she really think I wouldn't know who'd left a leaflet in my locker entitled *Bipolar Parents: What Children Need To Know*? Subtle. But I've decided to just ignore it, because I can't deal with another argument with a friend. It's tucked into a book in my bag and it can stay there as far as I'm concerned – all I need to know is that I'm about to commit social suicide *and* lose The Boy Of Our Dreams on the same night. Enough already. There's no point in having carpet if you can't brush stuff under it.

'So you're coming straight from therapy, Iz?' I say.

Playdoh Man gives her a little more room and we tut in unison, and then giggle as if that's just further proof that we're so close we're psychic. (Forgetting the recent lapses of power.)

'Therapy, then dinner with Michael, then party,' Izzy says. She started calling her dad 'Michael' a few weeks ago. She said it was 'something I'm trying out'.

'Oh God, you're going to be really late then,' I say.

'Don't worry, I'll be there to watch you pee your pants,' she says, deadpan. Playdoh Man is practically hanging off his seat now. I lightly punch her on the arm.

'Oi, don't joke. It could happen.'

Char giggles. 'Is that the time you all went to the audition for crispy pancakes or whatever?' she says.

'Fish fingers,' says Izzy, as if she's more of a grilled salmon fillet kind of girl.

'Well, *I* think Kass is going to be a star tonight,' says Char. She squeezes my arm and rests her head on my shoulder.

'All the same,' says Izzy. She puts her clenched fist towards me and flips it over. Out springs a panty-liner!

'You cow!' I say, but I have to laugh. I have to.

Char and I are as anxious as each other to get to her house without bumping into you-know-who; she doesn't know that, obviously.

'How's your dad been recently?' I say.

'What do you mean?' That was definitely a snap. Things must be difficult with him, poor Char.

'Well, just that he's letting you come tonight. Seems like a good sign.'

'Probably just wants me out of the house. Anyway, I don't want to talk about him.'

'Sure, OK, sorry.' Eggshells: everywhere.

We're at her front door and for the first time I look at the one next to it with an inkling of who might be inside. I try hard to think of him as Char's Dream Boy again. Only there's the yellow car.

No one greets us as we walk in, and I daren't mention Char's dad again, but I can't help noticing how different it is to walk into an empty, quiet house. We go straight up to her room. On the way I notice that all the doors are closed.

Char brings her room to life: turns on two lamps, opens the curtains even though it'll be evening soon (I wonder if she's looking to see if the yellow car is still there), puts the radio on. I flop onto her bed and kick my shoes off.

'I don't believe it,' I say.

'What?'

'The radio.'

'Must be a sign,' she whispers as the chorus of 'Other Side Of The World' begins. She hands me a hairbrush. 'Come on, then, practise.'

'I'm not singing *now*,' I say.

'In front of me? You're going to be doing it in front of loads of people in about two hours.'

'Let's not talk about it. Can you put something else on?'

She chucks her skinny jeans on the bed and flicks

through her CDs. She doesn't have many: her dad is very particular about what she's allowed to listen to.

'Westlife?'

'Those ballad-lovin', wholesome Irish boys? Sure, Sister Char.'

'Shut it or I'll sing the crispy pancake song.'

'Fish fingers.'

'That too.'

We're laughing the way we used to. Now I'm so glad I came back with her. Silly to worry about clothes and my usual rituals; I can find a way to do those here, probably.

'Here, have a look through,' she says, opening her wardrobe doors. 'Anything you like. I mean it.'

I'm missing the gene that makes girls totally comfortable about borrowing clothes from their friends, so I automatically choose items from Char's wardrobe that I happen to know she hasn't worn in ages: fitted black long-sleeved t-shirt with a tiny diamante heart on the right boob, black hipster jeans, thick white belt. I spy some white pointy ankle boots at the bottom. I can't remember ever seeing her in them before and I'm too shy to ask if I can wear them, so I accidentally spill a whole pile of things out onto the floor so that the boots are just visible.

'Char, what shoes do you think with this outfit?' I hold up the clothes I've chosen.

'Hmm . . . I have those white boots I never wear.'

'Which ones . . . these? You think?' OK, I am pathetic but it's working.

'Definitely. Go for it. Not sure about the belt though, babe. It's a bit "outfitty" like that. A bit like a zebra; black white black white, you know?'

'True. No belt. But then isn't it a bit black black black white?'

'Ah yes, but then you wear *these.*' And she hands me a pair of incredible earrings, with shaped and coloured beads hanging at different lengths.

'Char, wow, are you sure?'

''Course. You're my best friend, Kass, and this is a big night for you.'

'And you,' I say, and her smile is full-stretched and my stomach flips, and I wish we could swap places.

I'm downstairs. There is something very soothing about Char's under-the-stairs loo. Is it the beige? The sloping ceiling, perhaps, which reminds me of my bedroom. The fact that it is very small in here; a cocoon. It smells of vanilla. There is a corner sink no bigger than a cereal bowl and a round mirror that looks antique. The lighting is low; it catches the beads on the earrings. I look at different parts of my face but not into my eyes.

'Dutch courage,' my dad calls this; he's had a shot of something before every one of my auditions. But it's my neck on the line, and this time people I know are going to be there. There is only one bearable outcome of all the possibles: they think my singing is 'ironic' and I'm too tipsy to care anyway.

I was worried Char's dad wouldn't have any, but it

was at the back of a well-stocked cupboard. I took a miniature Christmas pudding as well, to take away the taste, and also because I absolutely love Christmas pudding but we never have it at home. I wonder if it's left over from last Christmas or bought early for the coming one. As I'm fishing the bottle and the pud out of my rucksack, where I'd stashed them in case anyone crept up on me, my copy of *Death of a Salesman* falls out and with it the leaflet Izzy planted on me.

Here in the vanilla-cocoon I feel compelled to take a quick look.

Chemicals in the brain that are off-balance cause bipolar disorder and its related disorders. But we don't know for sure what makes the chemicals go off-balance. In some cases, symptoms can appear for no known reason. In other cases, the symptoms seem to come after a life crisis, stress or illness.

Stress. There it is in black and white. And I know what gives Dad stress: me. And I know what makes Dad happy: same answer. So I can do this for him, can't I? I can do a simple thing like sing in front of people. How hard could that really be, compared to what he goes through with the chemicals randomly attacking his brain for no good reason? Plus he doesn't even have bipolar . . . yet. Me doing this tiny thing for him might stop that from happening. So what if it's only for now? I'll deal with now first and worry about the rest later.

I decide to read another bit.

Bipolar disorder may also be genetic or inherited. However, it will not usually be passed to children. About one in ten children of a parent with bipolar disorder will develop the illness. Nine out of ten will not.

I shove the leaflet back in my rucksack. Stupid thing. Why did Izzy have to show me this? Suddenly I wish I had listened more in maths lessons, but one in ten does not sound like good odds to me.

I unscrew the bottle top, pull my sleeve over my hand and wipe the rim: more a ritual than anything, because I highly doubt that Char's Evil Uptight Dad has been swigging rather than using a glass.

One big gulp of liquid courage later, the burning sensation turns to warm and it's sort of nice in my chest but still icky on my tongue. The Christmas pudding is wrapped in silver. It has a tiny plastic holly leaf and two red berries, which I slip into the pocket of Char's black jeans to dispose of later. It tastes so amazing I've finished in four bites. I check my teeth in the mirror and pick out the bits of raisin, then scrub them with cold water and my finger, and run my tongue around my teeth over and over. I stretch out the muscles in my face and breathe in deeply and look myself in the eye. I'm OK. I'm not mad. I'm all right.

Chapter Twelve

A Kind Of Frying Pan-Fire Situation

Dad and I have been texting each other since I left school. He's called sixteen times but I haven't answered. I've read all his messages aloud in a flat, calm voice, so that they couldn't wind me up (as much), and kept my replies brief and firm. Oh yes, I *would* be going to the party from Char's. And yes, with Char, not him. And no, I would not be wearing the cowboy boots, or the fur-trimmed jacket, or the 'bling' (someone needs a vocab overhaul). And yes, I was still set on the 'lesbian song'. *C U both there*, I ended with. *Just me tonight*, was his final word.

'My mum's not coming,' I say to Char as we walk arm-in-arm to the bus stop.

'Oh. Right.' She looks uneasy.

'What's up? Shoes hurting?'

'Yeah. Haven't broken them in yet. I'll be fine.'

I'm having trouble in Char's boots, too – my ankles keep giving way. Can't be the vodka, it was only a drop. I start to giggle as we totter along together.

'You're upbeat,' Char says.

'It's nerves,' I reply. She doesn't look in the mood for giggling, so I breathe in the night air to help me stop. 'You OK?'

'Yep.'

'Worried about seeing Cassian?'

'I wish you wouldn't call him that,' she snaps. 'You make it sound as if you know him really well now.'

'What? I'm just calling him by his name, babe. What else am I supposed to call him?'

She shrugs.

'Sorry, Char. I won't call him that any more. I'll call him . . .'

'Just don't call him anything.'

'OK, OK.'

Now that the good vibe between Char and me seems to have disappeared, I'm starting to feel sick with nerves. I was hoping to cover them over with some hyper girly banter on the bus ride; the kind you know must be irritating the hell out of every other passenger but it's so addictive and you're on such a roll that you just don't care. I guess you can't just make that kind of thing happen. At least, not when the other person has a face as long as a wet weekend; a wet Bank Holiday weekend, even. In prison.

We get on the bus and head upstairs, but it's so

crowded there are no double seats, so now we have an aisle between us as well as Char's black mood. I decide to ignore her and go over the lyrics in my head. *Over the sea and . . .*

'So why do you think your mum isn't coming?'

'No idea. Probably stuff to do for her boss again.' *Over the sea and far away . . .*

'Really? On a Friday night?' There's something really fake about the way Char is asking me these questions.

'Well, he's a real nutcase. I told you. He makes all these weird demands.'

'Right.'

Over the sea and far away, she's waiting like an iceberg . . .

'It's just . . .' She starts again; it's making me extra jittery. 'You'd think she could say no just this one time. I mean, it's a big night for you.'

I must be paranoid, but it sounds as if Char is slagging my mum off. I've never heard her slag anyone off – even her Remote Control Dad when he grounds her for the most trivial thing. Although, come to think of it, I did hear her slag *me* off earlier this week. Why is she starting with *my* family? Surely the logical thing is to start with your own and work your way outwards.

'It's not really that big. Mum's seen me do this a hundred times. She knows I haven't suddenly developed an amazing talent.'

'I guess. Still.'

'Still *what*?'

She's seen how stressed I'm getting and something in her changes.

'Nothing. It's nothing. I just think you need support tonight, yeah? I didn't mean anything else.'

'OK.'

Now there's Char's black mood, an aisle *and* my black mood between us, and there are too many heads on the bus and the lights are too bright to be able to escape into the view out of the window. I press the pointed toes of the white ankle boots together and look down and sing inside my head . . . *fire fades away . . . full of tired excuses . . . too hard to say . . .*

Char links arms with me when we get off the bus. I try not to resent it, but find it hard to drop this little grudge.

'Nervous?' she says.

'Bit. You?'

'Bit.'

We clock him at the same time, and she unlinks arms and stuffs her hands into her jacket pockets, and walks head bowed. He's standing in the entrance, behind Mrs Roach who is checking names off a list and collecting the £1 fee.

'Nice to see you, girls,' says Mrs Roach, holding out a hand. I'm tempted to high-five it but I give her the pound coin she's after.

'Hi, Mrs Roach.' Char and I speak in unison as if we're in class, and I cringe at how childish we must sound in front of He Who Must Not Be Mentioned.

Assuming he's also He Who Must Not Be Looked At, I pretend to be desperately interested in something over his shoulder and proceed to walk into the hall.

'Hi, you two,' he says. I'm not sure whether I should carry on walking, but I don't. I spin round and act surprised.

'Oh, hi! Sorry, I was miles away. Nerves.' I'm aware that I'm jiggling like my dad does, as if anyone needs a re-enactment of 'nerves' – yep, I think we probably all know what nerves are.

Char is dead still, right next to him, but looking at me.

'I like your boots,' he says.

'Oh, they're Char's,' I say. He smiles and nods her way.

'How'd you get here?' he says.

I sense other girls giving us the eye as they walk past our uneasy triangle. It's very much isosceles, which I think is good – Char and Cass close together, and me up here on a faraway point by myself.

'Bus,' I say. 'We came together from Char's place.' Perhaps I shouldn't be answering all the questions, but he's looking at me when he asks them.

'Oh right, I'd have given you a lift if I'd known.'

'No worries,' I say. Fine time to start sounding as if I've just stepped off the set of *Home and Away*. 'Anyway, I'd better go in.'

'Yep. Well, I'll see you later,' he says. 'Good luck, by the way.'

Char walks towards me without saying a word to

him and grabs my sleeve and pulls me into the hall. She looks intense.

There's a mirror ball spinning from the ceiling and disco lights bouncing off every wall; there's something that sounds worryingly like Eighties music coming full pelt from the speakers, and now there's a hissing voice in my right ear.

'I didn't know you were such a good flirt,' she says. People's faces come and go; flashes of clothes, shoes, snacks in bowls on long tables.

'I'm not. For God's sake, Char, you didn't say a single word. What was I supposed to do?'

'I couldn't get a word *in*, you mean.'

I clutch my head; I can't win here. Am I really that bad?

'What's wrong, Kassidy?' My dad comes rushing over. Just what I need.

'What? Nothing, Dad, why?'

'Your head. Do you have a headache or something?' He looks me over. 'You look all patchy.'

'Dad, it's the flashing lights. And what is with this music? No one wants this. People will be leaving in droves.' Why am I telling him this? I would *love* it if people left in droves.

'This is a classic,' he says. He looks upwards as if he can see dancing musical notes all around him.

'I like it,' says Char. She gives my dad a really weird smile, as if he's a dog holding up a sore paw. Even a dog wouldn't be dumb enough to iron a crease in their jeans, surely.

'Thank you, Charlotte. I'm glad someone around here has some taste.'

'She's humouring you, Dad,' I say. Oh, God, did he put whitener on his trainers? Blindfolded?

'Whatever, Kass,' says Char. So now my best friend is whatever-ing me. Bring on the karaoke.

Suddenly Dad looks like he's seen a ghost.

'Wow, it's . . . *amazing*.'

Char and I look towards the entrance. And there he is.

'Is that . . .? Dad, what's going on?'

The trousers are high, the chest broad, the teeth glow whiter than white underneath the disco lights. Dad walks towards him with both arms outstretched, and shakes his hand with the force of a bell-ringer. For one beautiful moment I think this must *all* be a dream. Correction, nightmare. It may have started in the loo at Char's – perhaps I drank more than I thought. Or earlier. It may have started the night The Other Cass came over; the night I went to sleep thinking about his leg sticking out of his little yellow car. Or earlier. The night after Char and I fell out. Or earlier. Maybe my entire life is a nightmare.

'Pinch me, Char,' I say. She does. Quite hard, in fact.

'*Ow*. Jesus.'

'You asked for it.' She has a point, but . . . *OW*. But I haven't the energy to analyse her worrying desire to inflict physical pain on me, because my dad is about to introduce me to Simon Cowell.

'Kassidy, allow me to introduce you to Tony.'

Who?

'Tony Ferrari – this is my daughter, Kassidy.'

'Pleasure, darling.' I'm aware that my hand is enclosed by some scarily hairy fingers, and that the fingers lead up an equally hairy arm to a puffed-up chest at my eye level and yet more hair poking out of the collar, but I am not at all sure what is going on here.

He is still shaking my hand and making me squint from the glare of his teeth – it looks like Dad used his whitener on those as well as on his trainers.

'Dad? What's . . . who's . . .?'

'It's good, isn't it?' Dad is open-mouthed with glee. With one hand he slaps his thigh and with the other he slaps Simon Cowell on the back. 'Tony has come to judge the karaoke. I found him on the internet. Wow, Tony, uncanny. Thanks for coming.'

'Delighted to.'

Tony seems to be a man of few words. I like that in a karaoke judge. A simple 'Tuneless crap' would suit me far better than an in-depth discussion.

'So, you're a lookalike,' I say, mainly because I need to confirm it out loud.

'Yes, but I do actually *know* Simon Cowell. I have connections.'

'Really?' says Dad, eyes popping out like a cane toad's.

'Sure. I don't usually bang on about it because there are some real weirdos out there, and you never know who's going to try to get closer to Mr Cowell through me.'

Sniff Smell fish, anyone?

'This just gets better,' says Dad, resuming the thigh slapping.

'If you're so connected, how come you're judging karaoke at a school disco, if you don't mind me asking?' I say.

'Kassidy! Don't be rude!' Dad puts his arm around Tony Ferrari. 'It's just nerves, Tony, she's not usually so . . . anyway, do come this way and I'll show you to your table. Now then, about these connections . . .'

As Dad leads him away, Tony shoots me what I presume is supposed to be an evil glare straight out of the *Simon Cowell Book of Facial Expressions*. It definitely needs some work. So here I am in a run-down school hall, with a phoney judge about to deliver the verdict on an even phonier contestant. Although she's never rescued me yet, I can't help wanting my mum.

It's seven-thirty and the place has filled up. St Agatha's girls stand in small groups and look longingly at St Jo's boys and the long tables of party food, neither of which we dare approach. The boys, on the other hand, head straight for the food and ignore the girls. Apparently this makes them irresistible, though they're doing nothing for me. There are flat cocktail sausages, crisp crumbs and broken biscuits all over the floor. There are small puddles of fizzy drink I make a mental note to avoid skidding on. None of the boys are house-trained, apparently.

I've noticed The Other Cass making his way through a packet of Polos by the entrance. A guy who stays minty-fresh versus some grubby boy who hasn't noticed a flattened sausage underneath his shoe: tough choice. Of course, it's not my choice to make. I'm only saying.

Char and I are standing with some other girls from our class. We are a mixture of *nice* girls who have never been very far with boys (even boys with weeping cold sores), *awkward-looking* girls who probably won't get very far until the boys in question are much older and less superficial, and *serious* girls who haven't yet noticed that being this age is all about who likes who and who's been to which base. We are the observers. We could write an essay on what it looked like was going on the morning after, but no one will bother asking us because we're just that bit removed from the real gossip. If I sound sorry for us, I'm not – in our school you're either nice or a slapper, unless you're really beautiful, in which case you get to be in a whole different category. And I want the whole proper falling-in-love thing, anyway, not some grubby snog during Spin The Bottle.

'So who else is singing tonight?' Char says. My dad showed me the list of students who'd signed up, demanding a detailed description of each person: looks, popularity, voice. I hyped them all up just to see how nervous I could make him. Anxiety makes me sarcastic. So now he thinks I'm up against a range of musical geniuses who look like supermodels and have more followers than the Pied Piper.

I point each of the Karaoke Kidz out to Char, with the name of the artist they're singing.

'Justin Timberlake, Girls Aloud, Will Young, Sugababes, Lily Allen, Beyoncé, Scissor Sisters, Nelly Furtado. And me.'

I feel a sudden wave of panic sweep up my chest, grab something in my throat and pull it back down to my knees.

'Oh God, I feel sick.'

'Just get it over with,' says Char. 'Can't be *that* bad.' Her mood hasn't improved, and I can whistle for sympathy, apparently. I wish Izzy would get here. At least I don't expect sympathy from her, and she has her own long-established brand of telling me to pull myself together.

'*You* fancy getting up there?' I say. I keep it light but I'm getting really fed up with her.

'*I* wouldn't do anything I didn't want to do.' (Says the girl who spends half her life in her room listening to Westlife because her dad's grounded her.) 'Maybe you secretly love it,' she says.

'This is my worst nightmare. What are you on about?'

She SHRUGS. Stop *doing* that, people! Shoulders, *still!*

'I just think that if you didn't want to do it on some level, you wouldn't. You'd say no.' She looks around the room and won't look me in the eye.

It's not true. It's so frustratingly not true I don't know what to do with myself, but I have to get away from her. A queue of girls desperate for the loo (or rather, the mirror in the loo) snakes down one side of the room, so I can't go in there. There are no other groups I can join invisibly – even if I lurk around the edges of one of them it would look like the equivalent of a warthog joining a pack of tigers, trying to blend in without getting its head bitten off. The Other Cass has deserted his post on the door, so I'd only have to sneak past Mrs Roach to get some fresh air. I'm headed that way before I've had time to formulate a plan.

I'm tapping Mrs Roach on the shoulder. Someone write me a script.

'Oh, hello, Kassidy. You excited? All geared up? Did you see Mr Cowell walk in? No bodyguards or anything. Your dad said there'd be someone special here but I never imagined it would be—'

'Mrs Roach, sorry, it's just that I heard someone . . . sniffing, in the loo.'

'Sniffing? Well, I expect it's over some boy, it usually is, Kassidy.'

'I don't think they were crying, Mrs Roach.' No idea where this came from, but by the backwards scrape of her chair I'd say it was working.

'What *do* you think they were doing, then?'

'I really don't know anything about it, Mrs Roach, but it sounded like they were . . . inhaling something, maybe?'

She's on her feet and headed for the loo before I've finished my sentence, but she rushes back to snatch the money box off the front desk, and, bizarrely, her asthma inhaler.

'Keep an eye on things here,' she says. Damn, now I

feel guilty about deserting her post. But not that guilty.

There's a light rain and I know I shouldn't be out here, not least because Char spent ages de-frizzing my hair, but the air cools my cheeks and finally I can take a proper breath, not restricted by the stress of tonight or the endless dry ice Dad insists on pumping onto the (empty) dance floor.

There's a crowd of popular kids about to walk up the path to the hall – fashionably late, of course, but not so fashionable that they could find anything better to do on a Friday night – so I decide to take cover round the side of the building in the long gap between the hall and the next-door sports block.

If I weren't so intent on walking straight in Char's boots I might have seen him earlier, but there he is, leaning against the wall with one foot up, his head down, taking a drag from a cigarette. I'm too far into the alleyway to back out now without seeming rude, or mad.

'Oh, hi,' I say. 'Sorry.'

'Sorry? What for? Come in, quick, it's dry just here.' He points with his cigarette to a sheet of corrugated metal bridging the two buildings. 'Want one?' He holds out the packet of fags and my hand goes up instinctively, though I'm not sure what instinct it can be since I don't smoke.

'Actually, no thanks,' I say. At that he toes his own into the ground, takes a small silver flask from the back pocket of his jeans and takes a sip.

'Sshh, it's just vodka.'

I watch him, fascinated. I'd never imagined him smoking or drinking. I haven't imagined him doing much, truth be told, except looking at me and talking to me on a computer and walking me to his little yellow car. Or sometimes banana.

'I guess you don't drink,' he says. He doesn't make it sound like an accusation, just an observation.

'I drink,' I say, and hit the ground with my heel a few times because I'm wincing at how hard I'm trying not to make it sound like a big deal. 'I had some voddie before I came out.'

'Well, feel free,' he says. Now I'll have to. Oh well: more courage.

The spout is so narrow I can't gulp it down like normal, and it burns my lips, but I take a proper mouthful so I don't seem ungrateful for it.

'Thanks,' I say. He puts the flask back and takes out the Polos.

'One of these now?' He takes one for himself and then so do I. We laugh as I struggle to get it out.

'Thanks.' I pop it in and lean against the opposite wall, but my feet shuffle around for the perfect spot and I wish I were wearing my own shoes; it's definitely the boots.

'Nervous?' he says.

'Mm, bit.' I try to reply without the mint falling out of my mouth.

'Must be even harder to do when your heart isn't really in it.'

Oh no, I don't want him to start talking about my

dad. I couldn't bear it face to face.

'Um, my heart *is* in it. I'm fine – looking forward to it!'

'OK, then.' He sounds like he doesn't believe me for a second but realises I don't want to get all heavy. Is he perfect or what?

'What about your friend, Char – is she singing?'

My heart drops a bit when he asks about her, even though I know I should be happy. And maybe if she weren't being such a bitch it would be easier. Except it's probably me, making her like that.

'No, she's not really into that sort of thing. She'll probably be a doctor or a lawyer or something. She's really clever.'

He nods. Must be interested, so I carry on but first I crunch my mint really quickly because I sound like I have a speech impediment. I'm sure I'll feel good about talking Char up in the end, though a tiny, tiny part of me . . . *no, forget it.*

'She's really nice, too. And *so* funny.' Am I overdoing it?

'Right.' He stops leaning against the wall. He seems taller than I remember. Or he's just closer. I'm too shy to look at him so I talk to my boots; Char's boots, I mean. Then his boots come into view. My heartbeat would rival a hummingbird's.

'She looks amazing tonight, don't you reckon?' My voice falters. I think he's going to kiss me. Shit. What do I do? I bring my hand to my mouth and cough, and leave my hand there – he can't kiss me if my hand is in the way. OK, carry on talking about Char, eyes down. '*Such* a good figure, and she doesn't even know it. I think that makes her look even better, you know? Because she doesn't know it, not like some people who are just so self-aware and—'

He gently moves my hand, and I look at him, and he smiles a You And I Both Know What I'm Going To Do smile. My mouth is so dry I lick my lips accidentally, and then worry about what a come-on lip-licking is.

Our noses are almost touching. I smell mint and then cigarette and I am giddy with nerves.

'Oh, Cass, I don't think we should . . .' Even I don't believe myself. And then my eyes close and his lips press mine and his mouth is so warm I almost make a sound, but I don't, I just kiss him back and let myself melt.

I have absolutely no sense of time as the kiss goes on, and on, though my hands hover together near my chest not knowing what to do, and it's only when I feel his hand move from the small of my back around my waist that I remember Char. Suddenly we are not a boy and a girl kissing, we are a boy and a bad friend; I am not one half of a movie-kiss, I am disloyal and mean, and I can't do it any more.

I squirm away a little and say: 'Sorry, I can't.'

He does the same smile as if I'd said something cute and comes towards me again. It's more scary than romantic this time – I'm out of my depth. I put my hands on his chest to keep a distance between us, only this time he kisses me harder and presses me into the wall with his whole body and all I can think about is this tiny hard fragment of brick digging into my head. I push on his chest but he kisses me harder so I turn my head to the side and say 'Sorry, no,' but his mouth is all over my neck and it's going way too fast, I'm scared and he's pressing me harder into the wall as I'm trying to urge him away from me, and then suddenly his hand goes up my top and I shriek, 'Stop!' and shove him hard.

'What the fuck?' he says, and what I see in his face is nothing like the boy I've been thinking about day and night; he is someone else, and I am someone else, and he gives me this look of disbelief and backs out of the alley. He turns and runs down the path and it feels like his hands are still on my skin. I'm frozen rigid in this moment, and the only sound is the rain.

Chapter Thirteen

No One Else Will Do

The doorway glows red, orange, green, and Mrs Roach is tapping her inhaler on the desk to the beat of the music coming from inside.

My senses are alive. There's the light rain on my face, the sound of tapping and of my breathing, and the sight of the moisture of my breath, and something new and awkward about me. The skin underneath my top heats up as if the feel of his hands will never go away, and I know that any minute I could cry, but that if I do things will start to happen; people will come over and ask me why I'm crying and then I'll have to tell them. I don't think I can. What would I say?

I can't go down the dark path now, the way he went, and I can't stay out here, so I walk towards the lights.

'There you are, Kassidy,' says Mrs Roach. 'I couldn't find any . . . *what you said*, but I did find three girls smoking, so thank you for being so helpful.'

'Sure,' I say. Red, orange, green. There are people on the dance floor now, glowing red-orange-green.

'Are you all right, dear?'

I can't get enough air into my lungs, and contemplate asking for a puff of Mrs Roach's inhaler.

'Kassidy?'

I think I say 'Sure' again, and walk towards the red, orange, green. I can't think straight. I'm here, I'm back there; it's now, it's five minutes ago, and I didn't just let that happen.

Everything is ruined. I feel like crawling out of my own skin and hiding in a corner, but I'm supposed to sing now. I'm after this boy, Justin Timberlake. Dad waves from behind one of the giant speakers, and jabs his finger towards the desk that Tony Ferrari is sitting at. Tony's teeth glow red, orange, green. Suddenly Char is standing right in front of me and for a second she is covered in black spots because I've been staring at the lights so long, but I blink and they go away and it's just Char, normal Char, the friendly face I need.

'You slapper,' she says. Is she talking to me? Does she mean me? 'Well?' She hates me. Char's eyes really hate me. I think if I try to speak it will come out wrong. I should tell her what just happened; why can't I tell her? No, Char, I am not; it's not what you think. I just shake my head and say, *'No.'*

'I saw you,' she says. 'In that alley with his hands up your top. You slag.' Do I imagine that she says, 'Just like your mother'? I must do.

'And give me back my fucking boots,' she says.

I look down.

'Give them back, *now*.'

I can't take them off here. Why is she saying this? I'm so confused. If she saw me, she must know I didn't want to. I was pushing him away. She must have *seen*. So why is she saying *this*?

'*Please*, Char. It wasn't like that.' My voice is like a whisper.

She knocks me as she storms past and grabs Izzy, who has just arrived, and drags her towards the loos. Izzy looks back at me as they go inside but I can't see her face properly. I need her, but I don't deserve her — Char wins Izzy's shoulder tonight, and now I have to get out of here.

I start to walk back outside and as the song finishes I start to run, and I feel the pinch of Char's boots as they smack along the wet pathway towards the gate. It clangs behind me and I'm out into the street. I keep running as I take my mobile from my back pocket and scroll down to Mum's number. I almost press the wrong button, but when I hit the right one I stop dead and listen to my breathing and the phone ringing and ringing and ringing, and:

'Kass?'

'Mum.'

'What is it, Kass? You sound out of breath.'

'Mum, I need you to pick me up. Please. Please come.'

'Of course I will, darling. But where's Dad? Where

are you, Kass?'

'I'm on the High Street near St Joseph's, outside . . . Boots. Please come.'

'OK. I'm leaving now. What's happened, Kass?'

'PLEASE, MUM, JUST COME.'

'I am. See you soon.'

When she hangs up, I breathe out hard and look up and down the High Street. I think I am myself again. And it's OK, my mum is coming.

Chapter Fourteen

Warning: This Phone-call Will Burn Your Ears

How ironic, it's the kind of night I love: the roads look prettier shiny with rain, and the car headlights stretch and streak into eye-piercing, beautiful rays of light. The *thud-squeak-thud* of the windscreen wipers is soothing, rhythmic.

Mum is letting me be quiet. For a moment I wonder if that's the reason I needed her so badly. There's a guilty niggle that if I could have chosen Izzy or Char to turn to, I would have, but now I'm here it feels right. Anyone else would have shaken it out of me by now, and I would have fought it, but we all know how much fight I have in me. (Even I didn't know how little, till now.) When she leaned over to open the passenger door I said, 'Please don't ask me,' and all her worry for me was there in her forehead but she nodded and patted the seat, and now she's driving and I feel calmer just watching her.

'Does Dad know you've left?' she says.

'No.'

She takes out her mobile and starts to write a text.

'Tell him I'm sorry,' I say.

'Don't worry, Kass. He shouldn't keep doing this, anyway. We've got to get a grip on things.' She thinks I'm upset because of the karaoke. Get a grip on things? That doesn't sound like my mum talking.

'I didn't run out because of Dad. It wasn't him.'

I have to defend him even though I know I'm dangling bait. She keeps her eyes on the road. Maybe it's her baiting me.

'Are you OK?' she says. And I know she means, *do I need to do anything drastic here or can I take your lead?*

'Yes. I'm OK. I just wanted you to come.'

She changes gear and touches my leg briefly, eyes always ahead. I'm seeing her differently tonight. Her quietness isn't weak; it's strong. She seems gentle, not pointless. I am wrong about people; that's something I didn't know about myself before. And as for how wrong I was about me – I have that bottomless feeling you get when you're little and find out that something special isn't real: Father Christmas, the tooth fairy, or the idea of your parents being perfect.

'Can we get a coffee from Starbucks?' I say.

'Sure,' she says, and pulls over. 'You feel like something sweet? Latte with a shot of caramel or something?'

That is exactly what I feel like.

'Here, put some music on while you're waiting for me.' Mum urges in a CD with a perfectly manicured finger. I wait till she's gone before switching it off. I'd rather listen to the rain than to Chris de Bleurgh, but it makes me smile, and I know for sure I was right to call Mum.

We park right outside our house and I feel like I haven't been here for ages. Was it really only this morning? I'm nervous about going inside but I want to, I just don't want it to be an invitation for questions about Tonight. I'm calling it Tonight in my head – a heavy but totally non-specific label that will become Last Night and then That Night, I imagine, because I don't think it will ever really go away. The coffee at the bottom of the cup is ultra-sweet but it's warming my hands so I don't want to let it go.

When we get to the front door Mum says,

'Oh, I forgot, Maria will be here.'

My eyes fill up and I look down at the coffee lid. But I can't cry yet. Maria is Mum's best friend. She is lovely, but I just want Mum to myself.

'I'm sorry, darling. She came over to babysit Raff. I'll get rid of her.'

'How will you?' I say. Mum is too polite at the best of times.

'I will.' The way she says it makes me believe in her instantly.

We walk in and I can tell by Maria's face that Mum must be giving her the kind of look that's like a secret code between best friends. But in her voice she gives nothing away.

'Hi, we're home.'

'Hello, you're back early,' she says, unsure. I just look all around the place like I've never seen it before. 'Everything all right?' Maria stands awkwardly by the sofa, groping for her bag without taking her eyes off Mum, as if she's been told not to make any sudden moves.

'Actually, Kass has a terrible migraine. I'm going to take her upstairs, so . . .'

'Right. I'll go. Bye, darlings.' Maria takes her coat and kisses Mum on the cheek and gives her a meaningful look. It's all very awkward but at least she's going. Mum steps outside with her for a second, and lets a thin strip of cold air into our otherwise toasty house.

I'm still cupping the too-sweet coffee as I sit on the sofa. I can see myself reflected in the television. Seems like it's someone else; perhaps it's just because these are not my clothes. I want to go upstairs and change them but I can't quite get myself to move at normal speed.

Mum blocks my reflection by sitting on the coffee table in front of me; takes the coffee cup, takes my hands, leans forward.

'What is it, Kass?'

'Umm . . .' My chin twitches and my mouth turns down at the corners. I feel like a little girl.

'Nothing,' I say.

Her eyes are already full of sadness.

'*Nothing*,' I say again, but my voice and the word don't get along.

She grabs my arms and looks intense.

'Kass, please.'

'I'm OK,' I say, trying to wriggle free, annoyed by the sudden demand when I had almost believed she'd let Tonight go. 'It wasn't . . . it was just . . . it wasn't . . . *I'm fine, get off, you're hurting me!*' I shout at her much too loud; I am not really shouting at *her*, am I? There's just no way I can tell her.

She deflates, she looks so sad and defeated; I feel awful for making her sad. Then she leans forward more, but it's too close, and now I can't look at her so I look down, but I can't look at Char's boots either so I look up and focus on the lampshade.

She just about manages to say, 'Tell me.' It's like a whisper, like she has to know but can't bear it. 'Is it about a boy?'

'*No!*' I start to cry but it's a sort of moan and I hide my head in a sofa cushion. Mum comes next to me on the sofa and holds me.

'Oh, Mum, I'm so stupid.'

'You're not stupid, Kass.' She says it like she's telling me off, but meanwhile she keeps holding me and I just let the sadness jerk my body inside her grip. I cry until there's nothing left, and after a few breaths I am calm, and I feel safe here with Mum. I feel safe, and sad, and stupid, and worn out.

Mum wipes the back of my hand with a tissue. Then she wipes my face.

'Thank you,' I say. She puts her hands over my knees.

'Did someone hurt you?' It's only when she speaks that I realise she has been crying, too. There's an edge to her voice now.

'Mum, I really don't want to talk about it. Please. It's nothing that bad, really, please believe me, please.'

I can see she wants to, but:

'You have to understand, I'm your mother.' She stands up and paces around and sounds pissed off. And that makes *me* pissed off because yes, she's *my mother*, and yet she's been letting my father dictate my entire life for years without stepping in and doing this sudden fierce act she's got going on now. She's *my mother* and yet she's usually so vacant we resort to clicking our fingers in front of her eyes. She's *my mother* and yet she strokes and pampers Raff in a way I can never remember her doing for me. This has all gone wrong.

'And whatever this was, it happened in the disco?' she says, like I'm the chief suspect instead of the victim.

'No. Look, I'm not talking about it. It wasn't anything; not what you think. I'm fine, really. I just got a bit scared.'

'You don't look fine. And where was Dad, for God's sake? What's going on here, Kassidy?'

Her anger starts me off again and I sob:

'Nothing! Please shut up about it.' How is this snowballing? Why does everything feel so horrible?

'I can't shut up about it. What's happened?'

'Nothing!'

'Did you tell anyone else? Did anyone see you?'

'Only Char.'

'And did you tell her? Why didn't she stay with you?'

I fall into the cushion again.

'Oh God, I've ruined everything.'

'No, no, Kass.' We are both crying, both soft where before we were hard and angry, but now what is going through my head is what Char said about Mum. *Slapper.* It's the last thing I can imagine anyone thinking about her. She's newborn bunny-wabbit innocent; I'm pretty sure Raff and I were both conceived immaculately (definitely in the dark, anyway). Mum turns me round and holds my head really tight to her chest. I don't want to tell her what Char said.

My hair is stuck to my face so I pull away from Mum and push my hair back, and give out big puffs of air and lightly touch my eyelids because I can feel how swollen they are. Mum looks helpless without me near her, as if she needs to be holding me. She gets up and paces, dragging her hands through her hair and wiping them over her face. I've never seen her like this.

'Will you ever tell me?' she says. I don't answer. 'This is very hard for me, Kass.'

'I know, Mum. I'm sorry.'

'Oh, sweetheart, what could you be sorry for?'

There isn't just one answer, so I give none.

'I'm going to my room for a bit,' I say, and I let go of her hands. I can hear her weeping quietly as I climb the stairs.

Everything is different now. This room: the sounds aren't soothing, the sloping walls seem lower. The last time I was here, I was different. His hands are still there and the tiny fragment of brick still presses into the back of my head. Will I always feel like this? No one has ever touched me before. I imagined it happening, a lot – even with him – but never like that. I tried to stop him, didn't I?

Mum is different, too. I've never seen her go through such a range of emotions so quickly. I've never seen her angry. I've never seen her that upset, over me. Over Raff, maybe.

Raff. I'd forgotten about him. Did that bat-eared pipsqueak hear us? I go back downstairs to the landing. Mum and Dad's bedroom door is wide open and the bed is perfectly made, as it always is (except for when Dad is low, when the bed is hardly made at all). Raff's door is closed. I try the handle. Locked. I knock. Nothing.

'Raff?' I put my lips right up to the frame. I have no idea what I'd say to him if he answered, but I need to know if he heard us.

Nothing.

I'm about to go down the next flight of stairs to sort out with Mum how to handle Dad, when I hear her talking to someone.

'She's upstairs . . . I don't know, she seems very upset. I just don't know.' Her voice undulates; waves of quiet sadness and rage. 'She doesn't want to tell me – I can't make her, can I?'

It must be Dad on the phone, and he will try to make me tell. I will never, ever tell him.

'I know, darling,' says Mum. I don't think I've ever heard her call him that. They don't have names for each other, just their real ones.

'I don't know, but I've got to sort things out with Paul, get him to see someone, stop all this from going on and on . . .'

Paul? My dad Paul? Then who's she talking to?

'. . . yes, I'll call you . . . soon. Oh, Graham, don't talk to Charlotte about this. Please. I think they've fallen out . . .'

Graham? What? *Graham*? Charlotte? Fallen out . . . oh, my . . .

'I don't know,' Mum hisses, like she's trying to shout quietly. 'I can't think about that right now. I've got to be here for Kass. I'll call. Bye . . . yes, sorry, love you too. Bye.'

Chapter Fifteen

I Guess Her Face Was That Pretty, She Thought She'd Get Another One (And Other Bad Jokes To Make About Your Mum Being Unfaithful)

'Mum.'

I've walked to the foot of the stairs silently, and I stand there and feel my socks smoosh into the carpet as I sway very slightly, back and forth, until I take hold of the banister. Mum spins round and holds the phone away from her as if it's one of Dad's socks.

'Oh. Kass.'

'Was that Dad?' I say.

'That? No.' Her cheeks are turning from Perfectly Pale through all the shades to Uncomfortably Pink. (If I don't mock her inwardly, God knows what I'll do to her outwardly.)

'Oh. Who was it, then?' I am praying so hard that she won't answer. I need her to lie to me so that I can get out of here – I have to go back upstairs and *take this in*. But right now I am on autopilot.

'It was Maria. I just had to . . . well she was obviously worried after seeing us come in like that, and – oh, Kass, I'm *sorry*.' Her face does that crumpling thing again, only this time I don't feel bad for her. 'I just had to talk to someone.' She looks helpless. Forlorn. Like always. Only she is not helpless, she is a liar.

'What did Maria say?' I can feel my voice giving way to my emotions, but it doesn't matter because she will just think I am upset about what she already knows I am upset about. We are both liars, then. *Just like your mother*, Char said. Char, my former best friend who is now not my best friend because my mother is a . . . no, I can't believe this. But there she is, scratching her head and frowning, thinking of the next lie.

'Well, she thought . . . she thought I should leave you be for a bit.'

'Really? Is that what Maria said?' When I say the 'M' of Maria my lips quiver together, betraying the tears that could come any minute, but Mum isn't really looking or listening attentively; she's twitchy, distracted. She just nods. Then she sidesteps to the coffee table and puts the phone down as if it's a loaded gun. I can see she's too scared to come near me. Maybe her aura knows that my aura is like an electric fence right now.

'I want you to stop mentioning it now,' I say.

'OK. I'll stop.'

'So you haven't called Dad, then?'

'I texted him to say you were safe with me,' she says. 'He'd left so many messages on my mobile. I was just about to call him then.'

'But you called Maria first? Dad will be frantic!'

'Well, yes. It was just . . . I didn't know what you'd want me to tell Dad, for a start.' She looks as if she's miming a rigorous hand-washing ritual, and the nervous throat-clearing has begun.

I could tell her that I don't even want to crack her, here and now, but that I can't help pressing buttons. She called Char's dad before she called mine. She called Graham Roebuck – tyrant, bully, nylon-wearing cold fish and everything else that Izzy and I have called him over the years – before she called her own husband; my dad.

'I don't want you to tell Dad *anything*,' I say. It's so hard to say these words, instead of the accusations I want to make, that my throat is starting to ache, the way it does when Dad makes me sing the same song over and over. 'I mean it, Mother.' Now it's my face screwing up – all it took was the thought of the look on his face if he knew what she'd been up to – and I have to put my hand out to stop her coming closer.

'No.' I breathe in deeply so I can speak again for a moment. My temples are pulsing with the pressure – there is Mum's secret, and mine, and they will both kill Dad.

'I really, really need this to be our secret, Mum.

Don't tell him. Say I ran out because I was too stressed to go through with the song. He'll believe that.'

'But, Kass, I don't even know what *did* happen—'

'*Mum*. It's something for me to deal with. I'm just asking you to keep one secret for me. So please, *please will you*?' I am practically bursting as I say this.

'OK, calm down, I will.'

Of course she will; she knows all about secrets.

'And Raff, too. He's not answering his door. You don't think he heard us, do you?'

'No, darling, he'll be asleep, I expect. Maria said he'd gone up to bed with a sore tummy. I'll check on him later.'

Darling? But I thought that grand title belonged to Graham. Charlotte's dad: The Remote Control. Everything that's coming out of her mouth is making me feel sick. How long has she been lying? For the first time in my life I notice the lines on her face. Her mascara has run. Her hair is out of place. She no longer resembles a shop dummy.

'Can I get anything for you?' she says.

I don't want to tell her that I'm hungry. It feels like I shouldn't be, after Tonight and now This. What's the matter with me? I think back to the Christmas pudding I scoffed in Char's loo, then the feel of Char's house creeps up my spine; the closed doors and the strange stillness. Now I picture Mum and Graham behind one of the doors. Were their ears pressed up against it, listening out for our footsteps? Did they smile at each other when they heard me go by?

'Nothing,' I say, the word jamming in my windpipe. 'I don't want anything.'

She looks at the phone and says, 'I should call Dad now. Don't worry, I'll tell him all this is about the singing. Maybe he'll even forget about the whole *X Factor* thing now, leave you in peace.'

She says it as though I'd be lucky for that to happen; as if *I'm lucky*.

'I don't want him to leave me in peace.' My throat is in agony, like I can barely get the words out, like I can't put enough meaning into them.

'But you hate all that stuff he puts you through. Don't look at me like that.' She almost adds 'please'. So polite, so soft, such *grace*; butter wouldn't melt.

'What would you know? What, suddenly you're going to help me out, are you? Well, don't bother. I'm going back to my room. *Don't* let Dad come up when he gets home.'

'I'll do my best.'

'Mum. Do whatever you have to do.' I stare at her so hard. Can she guess what I'm thinking? She looks guilty enough. I hate her and her lies, and it's all so messed up in my head.

When I get to my room I'm more out of breath than the stairs would have made me; it's all sinking in. The times she's worked late – worked late, or been with *him*? She's been coming home, cooking for us, lovingly prepared pasta and a big fat lie for dessert; we've swallowed it with a 'Thanks, Mum!' and out she's gone with a spring in her step from the new black shoes she must have bought to impress *him*. How *could* she, with that Cane Toad of a man? I feel so stupid; I feel the way you do when someone at school pulls your chair as you're about to sit down.

From my desk I pick up a photo in a frame that says *Best Friends*: me, Izzy and Char. It's mostly me and Izzy because Char's camera-shy, but she looks so sweet and she's looking at me like she thinks I'm something special – not the girl who stole the boy she loves, and not the girl whose mother stole her dad. We're all smiling – stupid, smiling girls who have no idea that my mother is about to ruin our lives.

I backtrack; I feel like I'm watching a home movie of my life when I picture Char getting on the bus, that first morning she didn't seem herself. That was almost three weeks ago – she's been carrying this around all that time. Why didn't she *tell* me? How did she keep something like this in? I can't ask her; I can't ask any of the million questions because I've ruined things between us. She was right – I'm just like my mother.

I put the photo face down on the desk and flick off the light, and flick it back on when the darkness takes me back to the alley. Toe to heel I ease the boots off, leaning against the wall, and put them neatly together in a corner by the dusty cello. I sit on my bed, close my eyes and rest my head backwards. I hold my breath for Dad's return, as if from up here I'd be able to hear anything but the wind skating over the skylight or the pigeons' babble. Instead I imagine what Dad might be saying to Mum on the phone, and her replies.

   – *I've been worried sick, Grace. What the hell is going on?*

   – *Calm down—*

   – *Don't tell me to calm down, just tell me what's happened.*

   – *It's . . . nothing, it was just that she didn't want to go through with it. The song.*

   – *She's never done that to me before. Not since . . . I don't believe it. She wouldn't run out on me like that.*

   – *Well, she did.*

   – *Yes but why, Grace, WHY?*

   – *I don't know.*

I turn over and press my face into my hands and cry noiselessly. I have betrayed my best friend, and myself, and I can never erase what's happened. Tonight I have fallen apart and I have no one, *no one* to turn to.

Chapter Sixteen

Oh, Brother

I don't feel as if I've been asleep, and yet the scratching noise seems like it's been going on for a while and I'm only just noticing it. Then there's a sound like a hiss. I'm on my back and the moon through the skylight looks like smudged chalk. *Scratch. Hiss.* I become aware of my fingertips and my legs and my eyelids, swollen and sore as I blink.

'Kassss,' comes a whisper. The hiss is my name.

Scritch-scratch on the door. It's Raff.

I get up and open the door before I've had time to decide whether or not I want to.

'Can I talk to you?' he says.

'About what?' Behind him the staircase is dark, and there isn't a trace of glow coming from downstairs. This usually means that Dad has locked up and gone to sleep. Can that really be? Did Mum fend him off;

and if so, how? I'm so angry with myself for falling asleep.

'I need to come in.'

'Raff, I'm not in the mood.'

'Yeah, I know, but—'

'*What* do you know? Did you hear me and Mum?'

'I swear I didn't. What, about the karaoke?'

'No, not that.'

'I don't know anything.' It's weird, he seems genuine. Everyone is different tonight. 'I didn't come up to talk about you, as it happens.'

I can't quite work out his tone, but I feel instantly guilty. Suddenly I see a thirteen-year-old boy instead of The Enemy.

'OK. Come in.' I switch on my desk lamp and sit on the chair. Raff is short enough to stand straight in my room, and he chooses to do that rather than sit on the futon. 'What is it?'

He blows out a huge sigh and runs his hands through his hair and over his face, as though he's doing an impression of some really stressed-out executive who's just lost a million.

'I need your help,' he says, raising his arms and then letting them flop against his sides as if in surrender to the worst possible scenario he could have imagined.

'I don't have any money, Raff.'

'I know.'

Now I'm really curious; I didn't think Raff could even pass a bowel movement without it being money-related. He's still doing the stressed-out executive thing, wiping himself with his hands as if he's trying to clean something off.

'Raff, I'm tired and I really don't need your shit now. Either tell me and get it over with or just leave me alone.' I know what I'm saying is harsh even as it's coming out, and I haven't got the strength for one of our usual rows, anyway, so I say it softly and in a monotone.

'I will,' he says. He puts both hands in his pockets and talks to his ridiculous reindeer slippers. 'I'm in a bit of trouble—'

'Oh, great, what have you done now?' I seem to have split out of my calm countenance. It's the Raff Factor.

He glares at me for interrupting and even I agree that it was annoying of me, so I mime lip-zipping.

'I haven't *done* anything. But me and Luke got talking to this gang and they want us to join. '

'You *what*? Why? To do what?'

'Wait, I'm getting to that bit! Just shut up and listen for once.'

That told me. It really did, actually – it's like I can't help picking away even though I can see this is hard for him.

'They want us to be look-outs on a few jobs.'

'*Jobs*? What, *crime*, you mean?'

'Yes, Kass, crime. Jesus, only small stuff. A few cars.'

'Cars? Doing what to cars?'

'Well, taking them.' He looks at me as if I'm the last person on the planet to try car-jacking.

'Right,' I say. I'm gradually swallowing all of this. I thought he just sold our stuff on eBay and used Mum's credit card. This is like some horrible flash of what being a parent is like. I am *never* having kids.

'But I don't want to. I mean, they're all right but they've done some full-on stuff that I just don't wanna get into.'

'Oh God, like what?'

'Doesn't matter. Just one time they really hurt this kid who was gonna be a witness in court against them, and he nearly died.'

'Oh my God, RAFF!'

'What? All right, calm down, *I* didn't do it!'

'It doesn't matter, why are you even talking to these people?'

'I knew you wouldn't understand.' His face screws up and he flops onto the futon, puts his head between his hands.

'What is there to understand? Just don't do it, don't get involved. End of story.'

'It's not that easy. Luke wants us to do it. He says if I don't he'll tell the gang I'm gonna go to the police.'

'But why would he do that? He's your mate.'

'Yeah, well, we had a big argument about it and he said he's sick of me making all the decisions and now he wants to be part of this gang.' He looks all hot and his fingernails are dirty – I feel so sorry for him I wish I could hug him. But then right out of my sympathy comes this anger and before I know it I'm shouting at him again:

'Well, what the hell am I supposed to do about it? You idiot, you deserve everything you get!'

'Shut up, Kass, just shut up,' he cries, and looks up at me with his tear-stained, grubby, hot little face.

We freeze to the sound of Mum's muffled voice coming from downstairs:

'What's going on up there?'

I open the door and shout 'NOTHING,' and slam it again. The contents of my stomach have turned sour. With me silent Raff carries on talking.

'I need you to fix it, Kass.'

'Sure, I'll just grab my AK-47 and deal with them for you.'

'Kass.'

'Sorry.'

'Do you even know what kind of gun that is?'

'A big one?'

He smirks, almost in sympathy it seems. One look at his grubby face and suddenly I am filled with the kind of love I know I used to feel for him, when life wasn't so complicated. I feel like I should have stopped all this from happening – how could I let my little brother slip out of our world and into this mess?

'I've thought of a plan,' he says, calming down.

'Me too. It's called telling Mum and Dad.'

Raff looks at me as if I just suggested he put on a dress and do the Hokey Cokey.

'NO. That's the last thing I can do. That will make things a thousand times worse, believe me.' I know he's right: we can't tell Mum and Dad. We need to talk damage limitation, and that means keeping this stress as far away from Dad as possible, especially now that my lying mother could have put this whole family in jeopardy.

I start to tug clumps of hair from the nape of my neck and focus on Raff.

'The only person who can stop Luke is his brother,' he says. I'm struck dumb. 'Hello, Kass? Are you listening?'

'Carry on.'

'I need you to call him. Say you've overheard me and Luke talking, and explain the whole thing. Say Luke's supposed to meet them on Saturday to agree to do the job. Fourth level of the shopping centre car park. Cass is the only one who can stop him. Luke worships him, cos they don't have a dad and stuff. Cass does everything for him . . . OK? Will you do that?'

My voice comes out stuttering.

'Why can't you? You do it, why, why can't you, why me?'

'I don't want Luke to know I've told you. It'll sound better if you say you heard us. He knows you're always listening at my door.'

'I do not!'

Raff laughs, but I feel like I'm going to explode with how awful this situation is.

'Chill out. Can you do it? Please. You're my big sister.' Great. He's played the Big Sister Card. There's almost nothing higher. 'Anyway, you and Cass are kind of cosy, aren't you? He told Luke he likes you. Good, eh?'

He likes me. He likes me so much he pushed me up

against a wall. I didn't think I could feel worse but I do now. There's no way I can tell Raff why I don't want to make that phone call.

'How did you even end up in this mess, Raff? How?'

'You don't know what it's like to be me in this family. Dad doesn't even know I'm there half the time. You're his little angel and I might as well not exist. It doesn't matter which of his moods he's in.'

'Look, I might have Dad on my back all the time but you've got Mum to take care of you. You've always been her favourite.'

'Maybe,' he says, eyes down. 'But she's been a bit busy lately.'

He knows. Oh God, Raff knows about Mum and Char's dad.

'You know something?' I say. He sits up.

'Maybe. Do you?'

'Maybe. Yes. Found out tonight.'

'Shit. Do you know who it is?'

'Yes.'

'Shit.'

That's all we can say about it. It's so unbelievable and so awful that there aren't any useful words we can swap. I can't bear to think of him weighed down with all of this. He hasn't seemed different at all, so it must be churning him up inside, curdling what little innocence he has left. He might know more than me about gangs and stealing, but what can he know about relationships and affairs and what it means for our mother to betray us all like that? I have to be the brave one; I have to let him be thirteen again.

We are quiet for ages, and then:

'I'll do it,' I say. 'I'll make the call.'

He breathes out heavily as if he'd been holding his breath for my answer all this time.

'Brilliant,' he says. And hands me a piece of paper with a number scrawled in black ink. 'You've just gotta do it by next Saturday.'

Chapter Seventeen

Spotless Kitchen, Dirty Liar

I come downstairs the next morning, and for a second I think I'm in that really annoying film about the man who has the same day over and over again. My dad smiles at me from the kitchen doorway as he wipes his hands with a dishcloth. This smile says, *I'm going to pretend last night didn't happen, just to freak you out.* Mum smiles at me from the front door, where she is opening the post. This smile says, *I'm guilty as sin but I can fool my daughter, easy-peasy.*

I can't look at her for long; I have to pretend she's not there until I've worked out what's going on and how we can stop Dad from finding out. He couldn't cope. This could push him permanently over the edge.

Raff briefly looks in my direction from his position in front of the television, Wii control in his lap. This look says absolutely nothing I can figure out, except maybe, *Oh, it's you.* The tenderness I felt before I fell asleep with my scared little brother next to me evaporates, and I make for the kitchen to distract myself with breakfast.

Dad hovers behind me with his dishcloth, pretending to have something more to do in our pristine kitchen. I'd suggest that the bananas need a polish, but I don't want to talk. At least I can be sure that he doesn't know what really happened last night. He looks like he doesn't have a care in the world, but he must be bursting to ask me why I ran out of the karaoke. Let him simmer; it's for his own good.

I think the toaster's broken – I'm sure the bread has been in there a good half hour with no sign of popping up. Dad puts jars in front of me – suggestions for what to put on my toast: peanut butter, Marmite, marmalade, honey, and there's also a jar of stuffed green olives for some reason. The man's a liability.

'So, a week to go,' he says. When I glance round he's rubbing a spot on the vinyl tablecloth with a dishcloth-covered finger. I try to remain calm and focus on the thin orange bars glowing in the toaster.

'Wasn't that Tony bloke good?' he says. I say nothing.

'Have the day off today, Kassidy. You deserve it.' Why do I?

'I know I've been pushing you hard. Maybe too hard. But it's only because I know deep down you want this. I'm right, aren't I? Aren't I, Kassidy?' He's looking at me like a child who's just overheard some awful truth in the playground and needs some reassurance so he can go back to The Land of Make Believe. How can I be the one to pop the bubble?

'It was my voice. I must have strained it. I knew I couldn't perform and I freaked out. Sorry, Dad.' I sound unconvincing at best, but his smile widens and he waves his dishcloth like a victory flag.

'I knew that's what it'd be. We'll go hell for leather with the rehearsals from tomorrow, but let's really up your intake of salt water. We can't take chances. I've got a new relaxation CD for you and we'll do those breathing exercises and . . .'

As he carries on talking I lean towards the toaster and my eyebrows start to heat up. Now my eyeballs feel hot, and the sideboard is digging into my tummy, and the combination of those sensations makes Dad's voice seem very far away.

'Sure, Dad,' I say, and the toast pops just as Mum walks in.

'Everything OK in here?' she says. 'Kass?'

'Everything's fine!' says Dad, and he plants a firm kiss on Mum's cheek as he leaves with a spring in his step.

'Kass?' says Mum.

'Like Dad said. Fine.'

I eat the toast in my bedroom, thinking and chewing and only half aware of the radio in the background. The volume on my stereo is on number 3 – it needs to be on number 4 to hear the actual words being spoken by the DJ, but I have no desire to turn it up. I just don't want it to be *too* quiet in here.

'Kass?' Something other than knuckles is knocking on my door.

'What is it, Mum? I said I was *fine*.'

'Can I come in?'

Instead of answering I make faces at the door, but I want to know what she's making that noise with so I get up and open it.

'Here, it's Izzy for you,' she says. So it was the phone. Well, what did I think it was going to be? Maybe a big sign saying *I'm A Dirty Liar*?

I mouth, *I'm not here, I'm not here,* and shoo the phone away from me. Mum tries to give it to me again so I shut the door in her face. I hear her apologise to Izzy and promise I'll call back.

We stand on either side of the door. My breathing is heavy and my heart thumps with all the anger I feel towards Mum.

'Kass, can we talk?'

She sounds so calm and concerned, which makes me even angrier.

'No thanks,' I say.

'I'm worried about you.'

Sure. That's why you're shagging – oh, God, I can't believe it; it will never seem real as long as I live – my best friend's dad.

'Don't bother,' I say.

'I can't help it, I'm your mum.'

Everything she says sounds cheap. I feel like ramming the door and flattening her with it. I want to scream at her until my skull splits open with all the pressure that's been building up since I overheard that phone call. A few miles away my best friend has this stewing inside her, too. Only, because my mother handed down not her skinny legs or her perfect hair but her taste for betrayal, we can't even console each other.

'Just go,' I say, spitting through my teeth. But when she does my rage deepens, and I move around my tiny bedroom like a caged animal, thinking of her picking me up last night when I needed someone I trusted more than life, and thinking of Raff with the weight of Mum's secret on his shoulders and thinking of my poor, clueless dad with his pathetic dishcloth and his idiotic dreams and his cheating wife.

I have made up my mind. I will help my brother out of his mess, and I will go to one, final audition for my dad, and I will never, ever forgive my mum.

It's just after midnight; I've been trying so hard to fall asleep that I'm almost groaning with the exertion. I throw off the covers as if it's all their fault and leave the room in disgust. I have absolutely no idea where I'm going, or what I'll do when I get there, but as I walk down the stairs the house is so eerily still that I get the urge to do something sneaky.

The hum of the fridge goes up an octave as if to let me know that it sees me here – that it has clocked me eyeing Mum's handbag hanging on the kitchen door. I open the fridge, take out the orange juice and have a swig from the bottle, just to let the fridge know who's boss. On my way out of the kitchen I casually unhook the bag strap from the door handle and go to sit in Dad's armchair.

Mum's bag is as neat as ever. She uses each compartment diligently, and they contain useful things: a miniature sewing kit, a packet of Wet Wipes and a packet of normal tissues (that's two kinds of wipe; is she prepared or what?), sugar-free chewing gum, a black biro, a red biro, a small notepad (completely blank), the world's smallest umbrella, headache pills, indigestion pills and a bizarre miniature toolkit with floral handles that looks like it was made for Barbie. All the items are clean, as if brand new. In contrast, no item can exist in my bag for more than half a day without becoming smeared in lip gloss and then covered in teeny-weeny bits of nondescript bag dirt. Pens explode in my bag. Things go missing. My bag is like a cross between the Bermuda Triangle and the tip.

I take out Mum's phone. When I say her phone is retro, I mean I need two hands to lift it. I go through her list of contacts; she has someone listed as 'G'. I feel sick. The number is a mobile I haven't seen before.

Her SMS inbox has only two messages in it, which already seems weird. One is from Raff. *Home at 5. Love ya mum.* That takes my breath away. I can't remember the last time I told Mum I love her. Anyway I don't now; I hate her.

The other message is from 'G'. *Sat a.m., my place. Can't wait. x*

Oh, God. I throw the phone back in and hang the

bag where it was before. This is a real live affair my mother is having. I knew that – I knew it before, but now there is real live proof, and a real live meeting taking place in a few days during which disgusting things will happen between my mother and that man. I feel like running up to my parents' bedroom and shaking my mother awake, screaming at her until all this pent-up anger is flushed out.

But I can't, can I? I have to think of Dad. All around me is the smell of the dying flowers he bought her: just a faint hint of rose, now, overpowered by something putrid. Why can't anyone else smell it?

Chapter Eighteen

Can I Have My Crappy Old Life Back Now, Please?

It's another Monday morning, and I'm standing in a very light rain though I could easily take refuge under the bus shelter. I must be turning into some kind of hair masochist – deliberately causing major frizz as if that will ensure that no boy ever fancies me again. Not that I needed any help in that department before.

On the surface everything looks the same, but nothing is. Or none of the important things anyway, but even the stuff that's stayed put seems unreliable now. I hold tighter to the railing when I climb to the upper deck of the bus, and check the seat for gum more thoroughly than normal. I don't do any of my usual thinking, either. I just look around, gradually taking in the objects and sounds that form my ordinary world.

'Hello you,' says Izzy. She's smiling but her eyes say,

Oh, Furbs, what have *you been up to?* I remember now that I was supposed to call her back.

'It wasn't how she said it,' I say, remembering Char stealing Izzy away on Friday night.

'You didn't snog him?'

I blush.

'No. I mean, yes, I did but . . . I don't want to talk about it, actually.'

Izzy grows even taller in her seat. I cross my arms and my knees clamp together; I angle them towards the window and huddle against it.

'Fine, we won't,' she says. There are three stops left till Char gets on. If I had the slightest clue how I'm supposed to feel about her I might be able to brace myself.

'What did you do this weekend, then?' says Izzy.

'Nothing.'

'Oh, right. So why didn't you call me back?'

'I just didn't. Sorry.' I know I don't sound sorry but I'm not in the mood to be told off by another friend. She doesn't know what I've been through these past couple of days.

'I needed to talk to you,' she says. 'About my parents. They're . . . getting back together and—'

'Ha! You're kidding!' I can tell by her expression that bursting out laughing is the least appropriate reaction I could have chosen. And, yes, I suppose it's not that funny that Izzy has just spent two years in therapy to get over her parents splitting up, or that every single day she has a new observation about why they were so

wrong for each other, or that they actually compete –
not just in front of Izzy but in front of her friends, too
– to say the most offensive things about each other. It's
not funny, but it is ridiculous.

I wipe the smile off my face; Izzy looks very grave.

'Come on, Izz, it's great if you think about it.'

'I *am* thinking about it,' she snaps.

'OK, sorry.'

We have to pause it there because we're at Char's bus
stop. Only there's a distinct lack of Char. I'm sort of
relieved, but now I'm desperate to know why she's not
coming to school – or not on the bus with us, anyway.
I half-listen as Izzy goes on about her loved-up parents,
and try to sort through the jumble of feelings in my
head about our mutual friend. It feels like I'm rooting
around a black bin bag full of black clothes in a dark
room trying to find something to wear.

Whatever she's said to me recently, I can't help feeling sorry for Char. Her personality may have turned
from fairy-cake to rat-poison in the last week, but she's
had a lot to deal with – that awful father (who is apparently irresistible to my stupid mother), and her mum
leaving them (at least someone's mother has taste), and
finding out about this affair or whatever it is.

But then there's the guilt. Because it's my mum
involved I feel responsible, not to mention skin-
crawlingly embarrassed. But then there's the feeling of
injustice. Char is so angry with me – she blames *me*! It's
fine for me to blame myself – that's my decision – but
it's so unfair for someone else to blame me.

Then there's the rage. Could this be the end of our friendship? This awful, embarrassing, unbelievable thing? And finally there's the awkwardness, because even if this could mean the end of our friendship, I don't think I can stick my neck out and save it.

So that's pity, guilt, injustice, rage and awkwardness: sounds like a pretty healthy concoction. Nothing at all to worry about. And as soon as there's a massive sale on at Allied Carpets I'll have something to brush it under.

I decide there and then not to tell Izzy the full extent of this emotional meltdown; I dread to think what she'd diagnose.

'Are you even listening to me?' she says. Oops. I really wasn't.

'Of course I am!'

'What did I just say, then?'

'Don't be like that, Izz.' I feel bad for not explaining why I'm being so vacant this morning, but it's best locked up. I just know what Izzy would say. If I tell her about Cassian coming on so strong: 'You owe it to womankind to see that justice is done.' If I tell her about the trouble Raff's in: 'It's the classic second-child syndrome.' If I tell her about my mum and Char's dad: 'Get it out in the open; you have to lance the boil.' (Urgh. I prefer my boils unpopped, thanks.) And if I tell her my fears about Dad, she'll tell her mum, who knows all sorts of people that specialise in locking people away for their own good and putting their kids into care – they've told me enough horror stories.

So I'll keep quiet about it all for now. Izzy would understand if she knew.

I walk the usual way home, and I'm so caught up in my thoughts that I pay no attention to the rhythmical *stamp-stamp-stamp* until I see Stamping Man almost bent over double in between two parked cars, pounding his feet on the road. My heart skips and I walk in a curve to get further away. His face is a blank. Why has he moved to this street? He's been stamping on the other route for as long as I can remember.

I walk faster, now in time to the stamping, now faster still. Even after I reach our road I can still hear him, though I can't be sure if it's a real sound or just my mind playing tricks. The more I try not to think about it, the louder the stamping seems. But what am I afraid of? The Stamping Man just stamps. And anyway, I'm home now.

Raff is sitting outside our place, eyes locked on his new BlackBerry – stolen, clearly, though he managed to convince Mum and Dad he'd won it in a raffle at school. He lifts his legs and drops them so his trainers bounce off the wall. I throw an empty Ribena carton at his head to test the hypnotic power of the BlackBerry. He catches it in one hand without looking and throws it over his shoulder to land in the open wheelie bin.

'Idiot,' he says. I can't argue.

'What are you doing out here?' I say.

'Forgot my keys.'

'Oh. I'm surprised you didn't just call your mates to

shimmy up the drainpipe and break in.'

'Funny, Kass.' He slips the BlackBerry inside his blazer and does me the courtesy of actually looking at me.

'What?' he says. Charming.

'Err, *nothing*,' I say. And with that scintillating conversation in the bag we head for the front door.

We both stop dead when we hear clattering coming from the kitchen, and then exhale tension like balloons with slow leaks when it becomes obvious that it's only Mum inside. She's usually home at least an hour after us.

Since Raff hinted that he knows about Mum and The Remote Control, I've been watching the way he is with her now. I can't see any difference. Either he doesn't *really* know, or he knows and this is just further proof that he is hollow inside. Or maybe he loves her so much that he has already forgiven her. I don't want to think about that possibility too much, because I have already decided that my relationship with her is completely over.

The clattering must have been all the vases – she's stuffing a black bin bag with the dead roses, and pouring rancid water down the sink. How can she do that and look so calm? I guess symbols are totally lost on her; symbols and morals.

'You're late, Raff,' she says, all sugary. 'You didn't have detention, did you?' Detention? Detained in a Young Offenders' Institute more likely.

'I was waiting outside. Forgot my key.'

'Oh, silly.' She tweaks his face. 'Why didn't you just ring the doorbell?'

'You're not usually here,' I say, not that she was talking to me. She looks over as if she's only just noticed I'm in the room, but then there's this fake smile.

'How was your day?' she says.

'Fine.' I try on 'breezy' for size, having done with 'surly'. 'Char wasn't there, though.'

'Oh?' says Mum. She's fishing for more, but pretends she's not by sucking on a finger she's obviously just pricked on a rose thorn. And she *still* doesn't get the symbolism? Amazing. She's cool as anything.

'We reckon Char's stupid dad has finally lost it and chained her up for good.'

Mum stays quiet. Raff nudges me and mouths, *No*. I mouth something else. He mouths something else, and I don't think either of us knows what we're mouthing any more, so he takes action.

'Mum, I really need help with my English homework,' he says. 'It's poetry.'

My little wind-up session is over. I can't believe he's on her side.

'OK, love, go and get changed and we'll look at it at the kitchen table while I make dinner.'

Before Raff goes upstairs, and when he's sure Mum's out of earshot, he whispers to me:

'You're still gonna help me, aren't you?'

'Yes, I said I would.'

'When are you gonna call him?'

'Soon.'

'Thanks, Kass.' His oversized bag smacks against his back as he runs up to his bedroom. Mum reaches around me from behind and squeezes me and I twist out of her arms.

'How are you doing?' she says.

What I want to say to her is, *I'm pretty much the worst I've ever been.* I also want to say, *I always knew I had to hold up my end of the bargain by not giving Dad any extra stress – it was hard, but I could handle it. I thought it was what you wanted, too. But there you are living some other life, and you don't have a clue what your children are going through.*

And just when I'd think I was done, I'd want to add, *What I really, really need right now is for my mum to chase away the monsters. But I'm on my own. I even have proof about what could happen to Dad now. The leaflet says,* In other cases, the symptoms seem to come after a life crisis, stress or illness. *A life crisis. Stress. What do you think you're doing, playing with our lives? You don't care about Dad. Or Raff. Or me.'*

What I actually say is:

'Tired.'

It's easy enough to shrug her off.

Chapter Nineteen

Simon Says . . .

I'm in my room, with a dull ache in the back of my throat from singing arpeggios really badly (even Dad struggled to hide his wincing). On my desk there's another glass of salt water, which will no doubt go the same way as the last one (into the porcelain wishing well). After the singing Dad wanted to 'work on your personality, Kassidy. Simon says he's looking for an instant affinity with the audience.'

'I hate crowds,' I said.

'That's OK, you can be the enchanting wallflower who blossoms before our very eyes.'

I knew it would be pointless to tell Dad that I had absolutely no intention (much less hope) of 'blossoming' on national television. It still amazes me that he can't see I have *X Factor blooper scene* written all over me, but I'm trying to get the balance right between keeping Dad happy and maintaining some vague level of sanity in myself, which means carefully guarding my privacy.

'In that case, I'd better go upstairs so I can practise visualising the ideal *X Factor* personality,' I said.

'Would it help if I invited Tony over? He said he'd help out any time. *For free*, Kassidy!'

Tony? Who the . . .? Oh, *Tony Ferrari*: The Doppelganger From Hell.

'I'm better off with a bit of peace and quiet,' I said.

'Right.' That got the thumbs up, and then he went shouting 'PEACE AND QUIET FOR KASSIDY!' into the kitchen and sitting room, for the attention of all two other occupants of this house.

Anyway, I'm up here now, safe in my turret with pigeon surround sound, but I feel so feeble and stressed out that the most I can bring myself to do is sit slightly comatose in front of my computer, drifting deeper and deeper inside the World Wide Web as I click on link after link.

I Google *Tony Ferrari* and find his website, which is bad on so many levels. Then I Google *tonsillitis* because Izzy texted me earlier to tell me that Char had it and wouldn't be around for a while and that I should get in touch. Maybe I should send her a two-in-one card: *Get Well Soon, And Sorry My Mum Is Sleeping With Your Dad*. I Google myself to see if any interesting Kassidy Kennedys have emerged recently, but all I find are the Kassidy Kennedys I've Googled before, who belong to Pony Club or enjoy running cross-country, neither of which I can identify with on any level, being someone who is scared of all animals with teeth as well as someone who dislikes breaking into a sweat/wearing shorts.

I've been staring so hard my pupils are starting to ache when:

stix: hi?

All these things happen at once: my heart stops – my left hand goes to my chest – my right hand presses the button on the monitor and it fizzes to black.

I just stare at the screen. Everything that happened comes back to me, only faster and with bits missing – just not the bits I wish were missing. My thoughts are saying, *Did you ask for that? Did you make that happen?* My thoughts are saying: *Why are you such a victim? Why did you let him push you around?* I think of that *hi* and the question mark – how can he be so casual? How can he even dare speak to me? Did I get it wrong? But there is no mistaking this horrible feeling that creeps over me when I let myself think about it. I know that I will never forget this feeling. I *hate* this feeling. I had hopes about falling in love and doing all that stuff and it being amazing and perfect, not being pushed around in a dark alley.

There are only a few more days to make that phone call. Right now all I can think of doing is hiding under my duvet and waiting for this nightmare to be over.

– *Dear oh dear, you look terrible.*

– *Lovely to see you too, Mr Cowell.*

– *Was that sarcasm, Katie? My, my, don't get too confident now, the audience won't like it.*

– *I couldn't give a stuff what the audience likes. And it's Kass.*

– *Fascinating. You're not going to sing for me today, are you?*

– *Nope.*

– *Thank heavens. It'll be painful enough to hear you on Saturday.*

– *It'll be more painful for me than it will be for you.*

– *I beg to differ.*

– *So do I.*

– *I beg to differ more.*

– *Mr Cowell, you're really immature for a filthy-rich music veteran.*

– *Don't call me a veteran. Makes me feel old.*

– *You are old.*

– *I'm never going to put you through to boot camp if you keep insulting me.*

– *I don't want to go to boot camp.*

– *Uh, why are you auditioning, then?*

– *For my dad.*

– *Oh, sweet. Sweet, and yet a complete waste of everyone's time. Especially mine.*

– *Whatever. I've got enough going on without your charming comments getting in my way. I've got to do something for my brother.*

– *Oh yes? Hopefully something that doesn't involve singing.*

– *I've got to save him from a gang of thugs.*

– *You seem perfect for the job, I must say.*

– *It's just a phone call. Even a monkey could do it. You could do it.*

– *I wouldn't be too rude to me, darling; you've been haemorrhaging friends recently without even trying. What's that all about?*

– *Only one friend.*

– *You sure about that?*

– *Completely. Umm, I think. I bet you haven't got any friends.*

– *If I wanted friends, I'd buy a few.*

– *Where from?*

– *Harrods.*

– *Good one, Mr Cowell.*

Chapter Twenty

Losing My Friends, My Mind, My Cool ... At Least I've Still Got My Hair

It's Friday morning; I'm on the bus. Everything that's happened lately seems to have suckered itself onto me like those molluscs that stick to rocks. Limpets, they're called – I only know that because we did it in biology on Wednesday. Otherwise I'd have forgotten. It's a shame I can't just forget what I want to forget instead.

Limpets can stay attached even when a massive wave washes over them. And if they leave the rock, they have a way of returning to the exact same spot when they want to. The spot is called a 'home scar'. So, even if I manage to get rid of some or all of my limpets, will they always come back to haunt me? I ponder this until Izzy sits herself down in front of me as usual.

'You look knackered,' she says, which is ironic because she looks like death warmed up (though still willowy and gorgeous).

'Dad's got me rehearsing like mad. I think I actually hate my favourite KT Tunstall song,' I say.

'Hmm, maybe you should have picked a song you already hate. Like Aversion Therapy.'

'Never heard of them.'

'It's not a band, Kass. It's therapy. Like if you hate spiders, they'll put you in a room with a hundred of them, and eventually you end up loving them.'

'Where do they get a hundred spiders from? Sounds bonkers.'

'OK, maybe not a hundred, but a lot. Or maybe it's just one spider, but you have to have it on the tip of your nose for ten hours or something.' Izzy makes her fingers wriggle like spider legs and runs them up her face and mimes a scream and we both laugh. I can't remember how we got on to spiders but it feels nice to laugh with her; it feels like it's been a while.

'What's your excuse then?' I say, mid-giggle.

'For what?'

'For looking like you haven't slept.' Her smile drops off. 'I meant it nicely,' I add. Obviously I should never speak.

'I'm fine. So what are you up to this weekend?' she says. She looks eerily expressionless now.

'Are *you* pissed off with me now? Sorry, Izz. I didn't mean it. You said I looked knackered so I was just . . . oh, never mind.' I realise mid-sentence that I don't want to get into another argument so I just drop it. 'I'm pretty busy this weekend, as it goes.'

'That's nice,' she says, with so much sarcasm I almost feel like rekindling the argument. Almost. Instead I just go quiet and lean my head on the window and stare out of it and drift far, far away. Izzy turns slightly away from me and looks towards the front of the bus.

'Here comes Char,' she says, and I sit bolt upright.

'Did you know she was coming today?'

'Yeah, she told me on the phone last night.'

I feel a sudden rush of jealousy when I think about Izzy and Char all cosy on the phone. All week I've been so busy rehearsing with Dad, or scripting this insane phone call for Raff, that I haven't had a chance for our usual girly chats, or even texts. Not that Char is even speaking to me but I've still got Izzy, haven't I? *Haven't I?*

'Why didn't you tell me?' I whisper, as the bus doors hiss open.

'Tell you what? You mean you haven't called her all week? But I told you she had tonsillitis, Kass. I can't believe you didn't call her.'

'Err, *hello*? Char isn't speaking to me!' And tonsillitis my arse, I might add. And also, *when* did Izzy stop calling me Furby?

'Well, *I* didn't know,' Izzy says. 'I knew she was upset . . . you *did* snog her Dream Boy.'

'No I didn't! I . . .' But I sense Char behind me and I don't have time to put Izzy straight on what happened, or why I haven't been able to speak about it, or what Char is *really* angry with me about.

Suddenly I feel like I've already lost Izzy – as if our amazing friendship has been unravelling itself secretly. I don't know how to wind it back up, so I just sit there watching my two supposed best friends having their normal, uncomplicated friendship, while I feel the pinch of those limpets and try very hard not to cry.

A few stops along, we're all quiet. Izzy looks from me to Char, and back to me.

'Are you two ever going to sort this thing out?' she says.

'Izzy!' I say.

'Well, it's gone on long enough. Come on. It's just a boy. You can't let him ruin everything for us.'

'It's not *just* a boy,' I say, but the look Char gives me stops me from going any further. I don't know what to say any more, to either of them. I can't win. So much for friends. I've got so much on my plate I can barely see over it: the stupid audition (Izzy knows how ill it makes me feel), Mum cheating on Dad (has Char even stopped to think how this might affect me?), That Night (and Char only seeing what she wanted to see, so she can hate me even more), and the phone call . . .

Here are my two best friends, scowling at me as if I've just started licking the bus seat. I'd like to shout at them, *It's me! Kass! What's happening to us?* But I don't, because I'm scared of being the only one who cares.

It's nearly the end of one of the worst days of my life, and I can't even hope for a better one tomorrow. Izzy and Char and I have done everything we usually do –

we walked to class together, we sat together at lunch, we went to our usual place in the far corner of the tennis court to read magazines, we ran alongside each other during cross-country – but it was all painful instead of natural. I can't look at Char without thinking about my mum and her dad, and she sure as hell doesn't want to look at me. It's mad to think that we both know what's going on but neither of us will say it. I'd never have believed we could be like this, but I don't know how to be any different.

I feel as if we all know that our perfect threesome is finished, but nobody knows how to break away. I bet Izzy and Char are just waiting for me to cut loose and leave them to it.

We're packing our bags with homework for the weekend. I'm already so behind with my coursework, but there isn't enough room in my head to worry about that.

'You both got clarinet lesson?' says Izzy. It might sound like a fair enough question, only Char and I have had clarinet lessons every Friday after school for three years, and we are both currently holding our clarinet cases – this is what it has come to, when we talk to each other like strangers. Char and I mumble replies and exchange very brief glances.

'Right, well, I'm off,' says Izzy. 'Good luck for tomorrow, Kass.' (At least she remembered.) 'See you later, Char.' (What? I didn't know they were doing something tonight. My stomach flips.)

'Yep, meet you outside,' says Char.

I can't resist: 'What's this? Outside where?' I just hope I sound more natural than I feel.

'Cinema. We thought you'd be busy rehearsing,' Izzy says.

'Yeah, I am.' I grab my bag and clarinet case and start to walk away. 'Bye then, have fun,' I say with all the enthusiasm I can muster, and I wave with my back to them as I walk out of the class feeling like the odd sock at the bottom of the drawer.

All the way to the Portakabin where the music lessons go on, my chest feels the way your finger does if you wind a single strand of hair around and around. There's ten minutes till the lesson so I sit on the ledge of a nearby drain, which is only a few inches tall but somehow feels better than parking myself on the ground. I peer into the drain – *whoa!* – it suddenly gurgles and I scramble to my feet, just as Char comes round the bend.

'Er, what are you doing?' she says.

'The drain made a noise.'

'Right.'

There's a tomb-like silence as I try not to think of all the jokes we might have made about drain noises back in the good old days before Char hated me for all sorts of reasons that I don't deserve.

'Did you do the practice?' I say, dipping my toe in the icy water that is my former best friend. Clarinet Practice Enforcement (CPE) is the only thing Char's dad and mine have in common (oh, yuck, until now of course, thanks Mum). The dosage they both prescribe is 'half an hour every day, before dinner'. The crucial difference is that Char makes the clarinet sound warm and chocolaty, whereas even after three long years I make it sound like a camel with bronchitis.

'No,' she says. This is a bit like discovering that gravity doesn't exist any more.

'Oh. How come?'

'I just didn't.'

I really want to ask her how she managed to get around her dad for the first time ever in her short but immaculate life, but I don't want to bring him up. But then Char has other ideas:

'I don't do everything my dad says, unlike some.'

'Since when?'

'Since whenever.'

'Char, sorry, but you *always* do what your dad says. We even joke about it. You know: The Remote Control?'

'Don't bitch about my dad.'

Hang on! Char made up that joke! I remember because Char isn't usually the make-up-a-joke kind, so it was historic when she did.

'I'm not bitching, calm down,' I say. 'It's what *you* always say about him.'

'Yeah, well, he's *my* dad. I can say what I like. Everyone knows you don't bitch about other people's parents; you just keep your mouth shut.'

'Oh right, like you did the other night when you bitched about my mum?' This is getting out of control. Stuff is crawling out from underneath the carpet: brush it back! Brush it back!

'That's different,' she says.

'Er, how?'

'I can't talk about this, Kass.' She's practically foaming at the mouth, but the other clarinet girls are starting to approach so I subtly *shush* her; I'm sure she doesn't want anyone else to know our business any more than I do.

'Don't *shush* me,' she says.

'Calm down, Char, I just don't want people to hear what we're talking about.'

'Oh right, typical, it's all about what *you* want.'

'What? This is crazy. I haven't even done anything. And you can't blame me for what . . . someone else is doing.'

'Someone else like your mother? No, but as I said, like mother like daughter – taking what isn't yours and then coming up with a bunch of excuses why it's not your fault.' (We now have an audience of eight. I don't know why I don't just leave.)

'Char, stop, please.'

'Why should I?'

'Because we're friends.'

'Right, like you're Izzy's friend, too?'

'Er, yes, actually, we've been friends since we were four.'

'OK, so what's her big issue right now?'

'What big issue? Izzy always has lots of issues, that's just who she is.'

'Her parents are getting back together, Kass. And she

doesn't know what to do.'

'I knew that!'

'Oh right, so you've been talking to her about it, have you? Comforting her? Being a friend? Having even the vaguest idea of how worried and stressed out she is?'

I put my hand over my mouth, maybe because I don't want to know the answer to the question I'm going to ask and I'm hoping Char won't quite hear me.

'Oh no. Why didn't she tell me it was so bad?'

'I don't know, Kass. Maybe she thought you were too wrapped up in yourself to listen.'

I feel like my insides are seeping out of me and covering the ground, creeping towards the eight girls with clarinet cases who suddenly know a lot of my business. I decide to run before any more escapes.

'You're all mouth, Kass.' Char's words feel like knives in my back as I run.

I get my usual bus. When it passes the stop where Char usually gets off, I feel a surge like a chemical reaction in a test tube, and I try to make it pass by racking my brains to think of the substances we used last chemistry lesson. Magnesium something and hydrochloric something-else: my anger and guilt making a bitter fizz.

Then the bus goes past Izzy's stop and my legs have life in them, as if they want me to get off here and walk to Izzy's house and beg her to forgive me for not paying attention. But the rest of me is lead-filled and I look straight ahead and then try to make myself believe that it's down to the bus pulling away too quickly that I did not get off and go to face my best friend.

I'm a coward. Everything is my fault. If Dad had paid more attention to Raff and less to me; if I had just made Dad happy years ago instead of resisting him all the time and failing at everything; if I had bothered to notice how left-out Raff felt. How could I not notice? And, just the same, how could I not notice that Izzy was burdened with something? How did I miss what Mum was up to? How did I misread Cassian so badly?

I have absolutely no idea who I am any more – daughter, sister, friend – I haven't got any of them right. The least I can do is make the phone call.

I don't know why standing in the street is the right place to do this, but I can't do it at home and there's nowhere else to go. I'm one block away from our street, sitting on a pebble-dashed wall in front of a house that hasn't been lived in for years, with blocked-up windows and a grey mesh bolted down over the front door to stop squatters.

Dialling the number gives me chest pains. I shudder at the thought of how much I would have liked to call him before; how perfect I thought he was, and how grateful I felt for a single word or a flirty smile.

I'd thought that if I never saw or spoke to him again I could bury what happened that night. I've blanked out things before.

But it's different now. What does it make me if I never say a word about that night? Or if I let my brother get into trouble because I'm gutless?

'Hello?'

'Is that Cassian?'

'Yep, who's this?'

His voice is cheerful. Somehow it makes me lose my bottle.

'It's Kass. Kennedy. I need to talk to you about your brother.'

My whole body is throbbing with nerves. He must be able to hear the shakiness in my voice.

'Oh, hey, Kass. Um, how are you?'

'Look, your brother is getting himself messed up with some gang and he's trying to take Raff down with him. I need you to speak to him about it. It's really serious, OK?'

'God, what? Slow down. I don't know what you're talking about, Kass.'

'Just listen, then.'

I know I sound more confident – stroppy, even – but I have to keep taking big gulps between each sentence. I tell him all about the gang and Luke's threats, and I even find myself confessing about Raff's petty crim ways and the fact that he's always felt ignored by my dad. Then I stop myself before I go any further.

'So that's it. Just . . . deal with it, OK?'

'Um, yeah, sure. I'm sorry about Lucas. He's not a thug or anything; he's just easily led, and Mum's a bit . . . flaky, let's say, so he's just got me.'

The way he talks about his brother makes me feel ashamed; makes me forget myself for a minute.

'Right, yes, I remember you said about your dad leaving when you were little.'

'Yeah, that was just *my* dad, though. Luke's got a different dad. We don't hear from him either.'

I'm softening – this isn't right. I don't want to chat about Cassian's family or his problems – that isn't what this phone call is about.

'I just want Raff out of it,' I snap.

'OK, OK, sorry. I'll talk to Luke tonight. He's in way over his head and it's probably my fault for spending too much time with the band lately.'

Everything he's saying makes me remember why I liked him in the first place. And that makes me angry.

'Great, so we have you to thank for my brother nearly getting his head kicked in.'

Silence. Except for my heart thumping. And then:

'I'll keep him busy from now on. He can come to our jamming sessions; hang out with me a bit more. Don't worry, the gang thing isn't happening. No way.'

'Fine. Um, thanks.'

And then it's quiet between us again. I think I can hear him smoking. I've picked a leaf off the privet hedge to my left and started making half-moon incisions all over it with my thumbnail.

'Kass? Are you all right?'

'What do you mean?'

'I just mean . . . the other night.'

'What about the other night?'

'You were . . . I went a bit far.'

It feels like my throat is closing up. 'You were a

creep,' I say. It comes out like a pathetic croak. I've got to pull myself together.

'I thought you liked me.'

I feel sick in the pit of my stomach. I wish I hadn't hesitated that night or worried for a second about what he'd think of me. I wish I'd shoved him hard the second it didn't feel right. I wish I had another chance.

'Kass?'

I take a deep breath.

'I did like you. But you shouldn't have done that. I was saying no and pushing you away.'

Silence.

'Admit it, Cassian.'

'Kass, I'm sorry.'

I wish he wouldn't say my name. I'm losing it here. My cheeks feel like they've been sliced down the middle with hot pins as a few tears fall.

'Kass, I really liked you, honest. I screwed up . . . shit, I really screwed up, Kass. I feel sick when I think about it.'

'*You* feel sick! Ha! Then why?'

'I'm not excusing it, OK? It's just . . . look, I want to explain but it's never going to come out right.'

'Say it anyway.'

'Fine. It was a lot of different things. The girl I was seeing last year dumped me because I was . . .'

'Oh, God, you mean you're a serial creep?'

'No! It was the opposite. She thought I was a bit slow in that department, OK? Shit, I can't believe I'm telling you this . . . it was not exactly a great moment in my life, being told I was backward – not that I'm saying that makes the other night all right. This isn't easy to explain.'

'Try.'

'OK, and then you said that the guy you were going out with was really immature or something – I know you could have meant anything by that but it stuck in my head, and there was that and the vodka and the whole flirtation thing between us and I just wanted to show you how much I was into you and . . . I'm just sorry, OK? Really.'

I don't know if it's OK, so I don't want to say it is. I'm so confused. It's like he's two people in my head – I thought the one I was falling in love with was dead and buried after the other night. This phone call can't go on.

'I don't want to talk any more. Just sort things with your brother. Bye.'

'Kass, wait! Hang on. Did you get the leaflet?'

'What?'

'The information about what your dad's got.'

'That was from you?'

I can't believe it. My head feels so messed up. How can he care so much about his brother, and now about my problems, and still be the pushy creep from the alley?

'Yeah. I printed it off the internet – seemed kosher. I just thought . . . you seemed a bit confused about what to do. About your dad. Look, his illness is not your fault. It's not your responsibility. I just wanted to help.'

This can't be real.

'I don't need your help. *You're* the one who needs help.'

I hang up and jump off the wall, wrap my arms around myself and walk quickly. Everything around me has an unreal quality, like I can't trust the trees not to fall on top of me, or the pavement under my feet not to crack and the ground swallow me. It was so simple when I could just hate him – not that hating him felt like a picnic in the park, but at least I knew what I thought. Is any of this even over?

Suddenly I stop. It's not over – not even the phone call is over. I forgot to tell Cass that I'd overheard all the stuff about the gang, so that Lucas doesn't think Raff grassed him up. But I can't call him back after the way I hung up on him.

Can I?

'Hello?'

'Um, it's me again.'

'Hi. Are you OK?'

'Just stop saying that! Ugh. God, this isn't easy for me, you know. I only phoned back to say that the reason I know all this stuff about the gang is because I was listening at Raff's door. OK?'

'Really? Why were you doing that?'

'Does it matter?'

'No, just doesn't seem your style.'

Is it pathetic that I'm pleased he doesn't think that's my style? Especially as I probably *would* listen at Raff's door? Now what do I say?

'Could you just make sure that Lucas thinks I did?'

'Sure.'

'Swear?'

'You can trust me, Kass. I'm going to fix all of this. Can I call you about it?'

I literally can't answer that. I just stand with the phone hot against my ear, staring at my shoes, just trying to keep my balance.

'Kass, I'll call you.'

I hang up.

'You're late, Kassidy,' says Dad. He jumps up from the kitchen table and stands there as if he wants to help me out of my blazer like some butler. I scowl at him, but his expression remains a glazed but jumpy sort of happy. He's going to use every ounce of self-control tonight in case he unbalances my yin and yang before tomorrow's audition.

'How was clarinet practice?' he says.

'Fine.'

'Did she keep you back for some reason, is that why you're late?

'Um, yeah.' Is it still a lie if the other person put the thought into your head, I wonder?

'Oh yes, what for? Does she want you to play lead in the next concert?'

I can't lie *that* well.

'No, Dad. I suck at clarinet, you know that.'

'You suck at it, Kassidy? I was hoping you'd have learnt by now that you're supposed to blow!' He arches his back as he laughs, and looks over at Mum and Raff sitting in the kitchen; Mum/Judas smiles and Raff hasn't even looked up.

'Anyway, come and have some food, Kassidy. You need a good meal tonight. We've got Chinese.'

'How come we're having takeaway?' I look at Mum, but Dad answers just as she opens her mouth to speak.

'Your mum was kept back at work today so she didn't have time. Here, prawn cracker?'

I take the prawn cracker but I can't quite bring myself to sit down in my usual seat between Mum and Dad.

'Kept back at work, eh? What for this time?' My voice is already faltering and I sense Raff looking up from his personal organiser. Mum fiddles with the back of her hair and says, 'Filing.'

'Filing what?' I say.

'Does it matter, Kass?' says Mum.

'Yes, it fucking does.'

'KASSIDY!' Dad stands up. 'Don't *ever* let me hear you speak like that. Do you hear me?'

For the first time since I found out about Mum, I have the urge to tell Dad. To hell with the consequences. She's making such a fool of him; the fact that he needs absolutely no help to be a fool doesn't make this any easier. She's supposed to love him warts and all, like I do – we're supposed to have that one thing in common, and here she is sneaking off every day with the nastiest man she could have chosen. Not a better man, at all. And underneath it all there is this niggling feeling because of all the times I've wished for a different dad – not a whole new one, but a seriously revised version. I didn't mean it – I want this dad; this dad who is standing over me waiting for me to promise that I will never speak rudely to my unfaithful mother again.

'I hear you, Dad.' I sit down and we eat tepid food with splintery chopsticks while Dad talks us through tomorrow's schedule.

'OK, it's 7.10 p.m. now, so that gives us twenty minutes to eat and digest our supper before final rehearsal at 7.30 p.m. Half an hour on song 1, half an hour on song 2, and then shower, followed by twenty minutes of yoga and then a ten-minute meditation before bed at 9 p.m. sharp . . .'

It's as if Dad has entered a speed-talking competition: he always talks quickly when he's Up, and even more so when he doesn't really want me to hear what he's saying, in case I disagree; which, of course, I do on every conceivable level, but I haven't got the heart to argue the small points. (As for yoga, he thinks I've been getting myself into the lotus position for a couple of years, but it's always been a way of being excused to go upstairs rather than suffer the horror of family life. It's not every fifteen-year-old who sneaks upstairs 'not to do yoga'.)

'. . . it's *very* important that you sleep well tonight, Kassidy, so I've taken the power leads from your computer and stereo – don't go mad, it's just for tonight – and I've got you these.' He takes a plastic box from his pocket: bright yellow earplugs.

'You should give those to Simon Cowell, not Kass,' says Raff.

'Sshh.' Dad dismisses Raff without even looking at him, and for the first time I feel what that must be like for my brother. I take the box.

'Your alarm is set to go off at 2.30 a.m., so—'

'What? You must be joking,' I say, and to my right Mum starts giggling. 'Er, what's so funny?'

'Nothing. It's just it seems amusing that of all the things to get cross about . . . sorry, doesn't matter.' She forces her smile to flatten. Ha. Ha. I turn my back on her and give my full attention to Dad.

'Right, back to it,' he says. 'Grace and Raff, I've made a banner and your job is to stand in line with us, holding it, so that we attract the attention of the cameras.'

Mum scrapes her chair back to stand.

'Me? I . . . but I didn't think I'd be coming. I mean, I've made plans. I didn't think . . . you don't usually want us there, Paul.' She grabs a tea towel and wipes her hands, then seems to stumble across the kitchen looking for something else to wipe away. Your tracks, maybe, Mum?

Dad looks like Mum just told him there'd be no Christmas this year.

'But I used the king-size duvet cover to make it,' he says.

'That was our only one, Paul.' She hangs the tea towel and grips the back of her chair. 'Not that I mind. It's fine. So, Kass, do you want Raff and me there? I just thought . . .'

'*What* did you think?' I snap.

'I'll be there if you want me,' she says. Doubtful.

'No, I don't want you.' I focus on chopsticking a cashew nut.

'How about me, Kass?' says Raff. Then he mouths when our parents aren't looking: did you call yet? I nod, and then say:

'You're off the hook.'

I get a cheesy thumbs-up. It's bordering on cute, but all I can think about is my mother going on some grubby date while I'm propping up Dad's mental health by volunteering to do something that has in the past made me so nervous I've wet myself. This feels like a whole new level of betrayal. She must really hate me.

Right then I know that this can't go on. She can't keep doing this. But telling her I know isn't enough – she'll try to wriggle out of it; she'll say I've gone mad. I need to catch her in the act.

Poor Dad's still talking like he's been mainlining caffeine.

'OK, Kass, it's just you and me. I don't want to risk taking the car tomorrow. I'll be too nervous to drive and you never know when you're going to blow a tyre and there might not be anywhere to park even though there are 3000 parking spaces as I discovered when I did a recce the other day but who knows how many could turn up so I've booked a cab with a very reputable firm.'

'Breathe, Dad,' I say.

'Right. I've made sure it's a no-smoking car and the

driver has a clean licence, and he knows the route to North Greenwich like the back of his hand.' Dad looks at me like a puppy who's just discovered he can chase his own tail for fun. He's even panting slightly.

'Good thinking, Dad.' This is all just washing over me now. I'm biding my time until I tell him I can't go in the cab with him. Watching Mum carry on with dinner, as if everything has gone smoothly for her, has made up my mind – I'm going to show up at Char's house on Saturday morning. Now I just have to convince Dad to let me meet him at the audition.

He gets up, takes something out of the back pocket of his jeans and waggles it briefly at me. I can only assume that's my fake passport. I'm not going anywhere near it. Dad puts it back where it was and then opens one of the kitchen cupboards.

'I've packed this cool-box full of snacks and drinks that will keep us going. Carrots, oranges, wholegrain cereal bars – I read somewhere that certain vitamins keep the mucous membranes that line your throat nice and healthy.' He rubs his neck as he says this, and I'm bursting to ask him how many carrots he thinks it would take to turn my reedy singing voice into something that human beings actually want to listen to. 'And, of course, we've got plenty of water.'

'Of course,' I say.

'And salt,' he adds. As he's checking and rechecking the contents of the cool-box, I get up so that I can put some distance between Mum and me while I put this shaky plan into action. I feel conspicuously unnatural.

'SHIT,' I say.

'Kassidy! I hope you're not going to swear in front of the judges tomorrow. It's not attractive,' says Dad. He's started to clear away the food even though Mum and Raff look like they're still interested in eating it.

'Dad, oh damn, I don't believe it. I'm going to have to meet you there tomorrow,' I say, doing my best frazzled face. Dad speed-walks towards me.

'What? Why? What for? You can't. No.' Great, he's taking it well so far.

'It's this thing for school — some of us have been put forward for a science quiz and we have to rehearse tomorrow.' My voice is shaking; the counter top digs into my back as Dad has me cornered.

'You never mentioned this before,' he says.

'Well . . . I only got picked yesterday, and it completely slipped my mind because I've been so focused on the audition. It's really good, Dad, there's only five of us being put forward. And it goes towards our final mark.'

'A school quiz? It doesn't sound anything like as important as the audition, Kassidy.' He's right, but I know what makes my dad tick and I'm one step ahead of him.

'Not just *my* school, Dad. This is a *national* thing.' I try to ignore Raff's look of mock astonishment over Dad's shoulder.

'But still, Kassidy, a science quiz isn't going to—'

'Dad, it's going to be on *telly*.' His face lights up. Bingo. There's a tiny high-pitched voice in my head telling me that at some point he's going to find out that this is a lie, but I'll just have to smooth that over when it happens. For now, he's happy.

'This is wonderful, Kassidy. I had no idea you were such a talent in this area.' He turns to Mum. 'I *knew* Mensa didn't have a clue what they were talking about.' Then he puts his arm around me and jiggles me towards him vigorously.

'Hang on,' he says, holding me suspiciously at arm's length. 'Shouldn't they have sent me some kind of form to sign? I know what schools are like these days – you need a permission form to blow your nose.'

I'm so close to pulling this off I've got pure adrenalin coursing through my veins. I feel like I could run a marathon. Or maybe the 200 metres, let's not be silly here.

'It's upstairs!' I say.

'Well, go get it, then!' he says, and we are both so wide-eyed – him with excitement, me with slight astonishment that I've nearly got away with this – that we must look like a pair of excited tree frogs.

I take the stairs two at a time; I'm almost blind from this rare physical exertion, but reach my desk and sweep all the rubble to the floor to give me room to think. First Dad gets me a fake passport; now I'm faking a school form. So, I've inherited his hair, ears and criminal mind – let's hope that's all. Permission forms – how hard could that be?

I'm so deep into my genius scheme that I don't notice the figure at my side until it coughs.

'Wah! Oh, it's you. Go away, Raff, I'm busy.'

'I just thought you might need these.'

He's holding the inkjet printer and the power lead for my computer. I'm frozen stiff with anticipation. The old Raff would have waved them in front of my face and then removed the ink cartridge and flushed it down the waste disposal. But this Raff smiles, plugs it all in and leaves the room without another word.

I take it all back! Cynical no more! I believe in crop circles, alien landings, poltergeists, the afterlife, and even in mascara that lengthens by up to twenty times with a special conditioning ingredient! I believe in miracles! I type Permission Form at the top, put it in bold and underline it. Yes! It looks authentic!

Ten minutes and two dodgy print-outs later I'm heading back downstairs. I pause on the landing to catch my breath and overhear Raff telling Dad that the reason I'm taking so long is that I've had a bad reaction to the cashew nuts and am on the loo.

I decide not to be annoyed that his cover-up is gross.

'Sorry about that,' I say, entering the kitchen with a rub of my belly.

'Kassidy! Are you OK? You look OK!' Dad is frantic.

'I'm fine, Dad.'

'No more nuts, you hear me? I didn't realise you were so sensitive.'

'Yeah. Me neither.' I glance at Raff and he winks. 'Right. Here it is.' I hold the form out a little way and then put it back by my side.

'Well, I'd better have it, then,' says Dad, and I hand

it to him upside down, as if stalling this for just a few more seconds can help me now.

About a week passes in complete silence. And then:

'Dear oh dear,' he tuts. 'That science teacher of yours needs to use a dictionary. Look at these spelling errors.' I take a look. Whoops. Apparently I'm supposed to show up at the science *departement* tomorrow for *revishion* and might be *appeering* on *televison*. 'But it does sound like an experience we can't let you miss out on,' he says. Sometimes it works in my favour that Dad is blind to my flaws.

Now he slopes over to the sofa and slumps down.

'What are we going to do about *The X Factor*, Kassidy?'

'Hang on,' says Mum, still over at the table. All three of us turn sharply: the tone of her voice was different, commanding. It doesn't take a genius to work out where she's picked *that* up.

'What is it?' says Dad.

'I just think we need to consider what Kass wants, Paul. Is she really going to feel like dashing from a tele-vised science quiz to a televised audition? Let's let *her* make the decisions here.' It's like *Invasion of the Body Snatchers*. What's she going to come out with next? *Where ya gonna go? Where ya gonna run? Where ya gonna hide?* It's like having Graham actually in the room. I feel oddly powerful knowing that she has no clue what I'm really up to. She's about to seal her own fate.

'Yes, let's let me make the decision,' I say. I sit next to Dad and put my arm around him. 'It's fine, Dad. I can meet you in the queue.' I give Mum a warning glance not to interrupt again. She looks so worried about me; oh sure, *now* she's worried. It's Dad she should be worried about. And herself.

'There's a tube to North Greenwich and you know how long it's going to take to get inside and get a number and everything – it's probably best if I'm not out in the cold air all that time.'

'She's right, Dad,' says Raff. I could almost get to like him. 'Plus if Kass is concentrating on science all day she won't have time to get nervous about the audition. And you know what happens when she gets nervous.'

Ah, he's still Raff underneath this strange new disguise.

'I suppose,' says Dad. 'You promise you'll come straight to the O2 afterwards? But how will you find me?'

'Easy. Mobiles.'

Mum comes over to our cosy gang of three.

'So everyone's happy?' she says.

The feel of her behind me makes my skin crawl. Dad looks at me, all serious, and then his face breaks into a huge smile.

'I'm so proud of you, Kassidy,' he says. I hug him quickly before he sees how guilty I look, and how much he breaks my heart.

– You again. What, couldn't find anyone else to hang out with?

– *Of course I could. I can't choose my dreams, you know. They just happen. You're the last person I want to spend time with, remember?*

– *Darling, I may be the only person left who's still listening to you.*

– *Err, no.*

– *I beg to differ. Char obviously can't stand the sight of you. Izzy didn't even tell you she was majorly stressed out over her parents. Raff's only using you. Your mother's too busy being amorous. And your father – well, he's never listened to you.*

– *S'pose.*

– *Oh no, don't get all glum now.*

– *I'll try. Mr Cowell?*

– *Yes, Kass?*

– *I'm scared.*

– *Of me?*

– *No. Funny, you're about the only thing I'm not scared of.*

Chapter Twenty-One

Marriage Counselling For Beginners

I'm on Char's street, shrouded between a disused phone box and a privet hedge, and slightly over-dressed for spying in my audition outfit: fitted Rolling Stones T-shirt featuring giant red sparkly lips, little black waistcoat, skinny jeans and ankle boots, with huge hoop earrings that keep getting tangled in my hair, and plenty of face on. I've overdone it with the lip gloss – I feel like I've dipped my mouth in a jar of honey.

While I'm wiping it off with a tissue I spy Char and Izzy leaving Char's house. They walk arm in arm away from me, one about a foot taller than the other, deep in the excited chatter of pre-shopping-trip girls. That used to be a three-of-us ritual, every Saturday morning.

My mobile vibrates in my back pocket. It'll be Dad wanting to give me some last-minute science facts or to tell me again not to swear on telly.

It's not Dad. It's Cassian. I don't know what to do –
where's the pause button? I need time to think about
whether or not to answer.

Too late: it goes to voicemail.

'Hi, Kass, it's just me. I wanted to talk to you about
the Lucas thing. Call me. Um, please. Cheers. Bye.'

He sounds kind of nervous in the message, and it
reminds me of that time he stumbled on the kerb outside my house. It makes me think that I'm always so
preoccupied with my own stumbling that I forget that
other people might not find life any easier than I do.

I'm calling him.

'Kass?'

'Yep. Hi. I got your message.'

'Great. So I spoke to my brother. It got a bit out of
hand, but everything's cool now.'

'What do you mean, it got out of hand?'

'Um, he punched me.' He kind of laughs. 'Bloody
hurt actually, but I think he just needed to do it.'

'God. Um, OK, and then what?'

'So then we talked a lot. I won't bore you with all the
details but I asked him to join the band – kind of an
assistant roadie – and he swears he's not getting
involved in the gang. I'm gonna keep a closer eye on
him. So, are we cool?'

'What do you mean?'

'I dunno. Are you OK about this Raff and Lucas
thing?'

'Sure, yes. I'm fine. Thanks for sorting it out.'

And then it's awkward. He says:

'Are you at home?'

'Yep. Are you?'

'Yep, just leaving – for the audition. You?'

'Yep, just leaving.'

I peer around the phone box and imagine him in his house, maybe in his room, maybe at his drum kit, speaking to me.

'Kass? Is there any chance we could . . .?'

'I don't think so.'

That's hard to say when I still have feelings for him, but I know it's right. I can't go back. He's not the Bad Guy I thought he was, but I can't just forget it.

'But Cass? Thanks for the leaflet and everything. I think you're a . . . nice guy.'

'I'm really glad you think so. But, really really never? For us, I mean?'

'How about friends?'

I wait about a week for him to answer.

'Friends is good. OK, gotta go. I guess I might see you in the queue, hey?'

I laugh.

'That seems likely with about a million people there.'

He laughs. Maybe we really will be friends. I could use some, that's for sure.

'Seeya, Kass.'

'Seeya, Cass.'

We both laugh as we hang up.

About a minute later it's back to reality as I hear the *clip-clip-scrape-clip* of high heels, and I know without looking that it's my mother. I peer round. She opens the gate and walks up the path to Char's house as if she owns the place. He must have been waiting for her by the door because she walks straight in. I feel like my insides are on fire. What am I doing here? I am so riddled with nerves and bursting with purpose: this could go either way – *I* could go either way. Run away, or deal with it.

I'm at the front door, breathing in through my nose, and out through my mouth – finally Dad's breathing exercises are coming in handy. The doorbell chimes in that familiar way and I have to steady myself by holding onto the porch.

I know Graham will answer; I bet he'll pretend he doesn't know who I am. As I wait I mutter an imaginary conversation to calm my nerves:

– *One of Charlotte's friends, are you?*
– *Well, I'm not the postman, Mr Roebuck.*
– *Sorry, still can't place you.*
– *Tell you what, add thirty years and imagine me in something beige from Marks and Spencers. That might ring a bell.*

But that's where the script ends; everything else I say will have to be improvised. I only know that I mustn't cry or seem like a baby, or have him pity me – I've got to stay in control and get my points across.

This is taking ages; I dread to think why. As I crouch down and look through the letter box, I get an eyeful of navy trousers and spring upright as the door opens.

'Oh. Kass.' He doesn't sound cold and hard like normal; there is warmth in that just-seen-a-ghost expression. It makes me feel sick.

'Can I come in?' I say. I'm quite surprised by how forceful I sound.

'Charlotte isn't here.'

'I know. I've come to see you.' I try to look over his shoulder when I hear the sound of the loo flushing, and he moves to block me.

'Kass, I think you should go,' he says, putting a hand up like a power-crazy traffic policeman.

'Is that my mum?' I try to step forward, but he puts his arm on the door frame, so I hang onto it and try to budge him. 'Mum!'

She comes out of the downstairs loo where I drank the vodka and ate the Christmas pudding. She clutches her chest when she sees me and stumbles back against the wall, letting out a kind of tragic moan. Then, as if she's been reprogrammed by the Robot Master, she straightens up and smoothes her hair and comes towards the door.

'Kass, hi, what a surprise. I came to pick you up but you weren't here!'

Is she kidding? She must think I was born yesterday.

'I never said I was going to be here.'

Remote Control's arm is still blocking me, until Mum comes right to the door. The sight of them together makes my legs go wobbly.

'Oh, didn't you? I could have sworn you said you

were heading to Char's right before the science quiz. And here you are. So, shall we go?'

She's unbelievable; only she's not, she's good, she's really good – if I didn't already know for sure what a lying cow she is I'd have been sucked in.

'I never said I was heading to Char's.' I can't quite bear to blurt out that I know everything; slow and painful seems preferable somehow. 'I'm supposed to be meeting Dad for the audition, remember?'

'Of course you are! Well, come on, we'd better get going. I've got the car, so I'll race you over there. Thanks, Graham, we'd better be off.'

He looks bewildered. She grabs her coat and bag and comes towards me, but this time *I* block the way with my arm on the door frame.

'That was pathetic,' I say, almost at a whisper.

'Come on, Kass,' she says, pretending she didn't hear me, 'let's get going.'

'No,' I say, and her chin trembles and she puts her hand over her mouth and runs back into the house, crying.

We're at the kitchen table; the three of us. I feel like this is Mum and Char's dad as a unit, and me the outsider; maybe because they're sitting in identical positions with their hands clasped together, placed on their lips, and their elbows on the table, and both staring at me. I almost wish Char was here. Or rather, I wish Char was here and that she didn't hate me.

'Well, is one of you going to speak?' I say. I can't

believe how angry I feel; I'm not even close to crying.

'Kass,' begins Char's dad, lowering his clasped hands.

'Not you,' I snap, and then I look at Mum. Her whole face starts twitching and she bursts into tears again.

'Oh, darling, I'm so sorry. I never wanted this.'

'What? To get found out? Well you did a pretty shit job then, because *I* know, *Raff* knows—'

'Raff? Oh, God, please no.' Mum turns briefly to Char's dad, and for a second I get distracted by the jealous thought that now she's more concerned about Raff's feelings than mine. But then I feel protective of him again and the jealousy gets shunted back where it belongs.

'And Char knows,' I say to her dad. He closes his eyes and lowers his head and I notice for the first time that he has a bald patch. My dad doesn't have a bald patch. He doesn't wear polyester trousers and nasty grey shoes, either. *And* he doesn't have hairy fingers. If it's possible, I have even less respect for my mother now.

I'm starting to get annoyed by how quiet they're being. I don't know what I expected (that's what happens when your natural tendency is to do things without thinking them through, I suppose), but the rage bubbling inside me doesn't seem compatible with how calm they seem, despite my mother's quivering chin and tendency to let out little bursts of gentle crying.

'So, what is this . . . *this*?' I say, wagging my finger

back and forth between them. I know how bold I must sound, though inside I'm still wondering when I'm going to get told off for being so cheeky. But they're both so meek, so guilty, it's like I have no choice.

They shrug awkwardly as if they have itching powder in their matching beige jumpers. Then Mum straightens up and sniffs. She's done with crying and has pulled herself together. At last it seems I might get some answers.

'To be honest, Kass, I don't know.'

Char's dad looks at her like this is news to him. Mum won't meet his gaze.

'I wasn't really thinking about what it was . . . is . . . was, whatever, sorry. Sorry, Graham.'

'Don't apologise to him! Why would you apologise to him? I can't believe this. What's the matter with you?'

'Don't speak to me like that, Kassidy.' She smacks the table and stands.

'It's Kass.'

'It's KASSIDY, actually, I'm your mother and that's the name I gave you.'

Graham gets up and, with all ten fingertips placed lightly on the table, as if he's afraid it might levitate, he speaks very calmly:

'I'm going to leave you two for a minute. I'll just be in the lounge.'

Mum doesn't bat an eyelid; she's still fuming over what I said. Unbelievable! She's got the nerve to get angry with me. I didn't even know she had . . . *nerve*. Well, guess what? Me too.

'Don't shout at me.' I stand so I'm on her level. '*You're* the one who's betrayed everyone. *You're* the one who's ruined my friendships and let your children down and cheated on Dad. How could you do that to him? He loves you.'

'No, he doesn't! He doesn't even know I'm there. I'm invisible; I'm nothing. You don't know what you're saying. You don't know anything about this. What do *you* know about marriage?'

'Err, I know you're supposed to be *faithful*. I know you're not supposed to *shag* your daughter's best friend's dad.'

The slap across my face and the look of rage on Mum's face stops me dead.

'Oh, God, I'm sorry, Kass,' she says. 'I'm so sorry, but you're not being fair – I know how awful this must seem but you don't understand. You *couldn't* understand what it's like to be me.'

I just hold my cheek as my eyes fill with tears, and she carries on:

'I go to work every day and I'm the dogsbody, the one who does what nobody else thinks themselves low enough to do, and I don't get thanked for it. Then I come home and I tread on eggshells in front of your father in case he . . . flips. And meanwhile I'm getting it in the neck from you and your brother for not buying the right crisps or cooking the right meal or ironing the right shirt, or for nagging, or for just being a rubbish mum. And you know what, Kass? Just for a change I wanted to spend some time with a grown-up who doesn't really *need* me but really *wants* me. And who thinks I'm OK. I'm not so bad.'

She slumps back into the chair and resumes her position of elbows on table, clasped hands in front of mouth. She's shaking.

'Please, Kass, sit down.'

But what could I possibly say? And how much more can I bear to listen to? I can't fix this; I don't know why I thought I could.

Without another word I walk out of the kitchen and down the hall, catching a glimpse of Graham standing thoughtfully by the mantelpiece and a photograph of Char. I walk out, leaving the door wide open.

Somewhere in a queue in North Greenwich Stadium, Dad is waiting.

Chapter Twenty-Two

This Train Terminates At . . .

It may be because I've used up my entire sense of purpose that it takes me two hours to reach the Tube station – a fifteen-minute walk, usually. It's as if there's an invisible force field around it, repelling me. I've been into three cafés and two bookshops. I've cried in a phone box and used the loo in McDonald's to fix my make-up.

Now I'm down here in the station. It's a milestone. I've been standing in front of the Tube map long enough to memorise the whole thing; I can't walk away until I'm absolutely sure which route to take. This way takes ten stops with two changes; that way takes nine stops with three changes. Just when I think I've decided and let my eyes drift up the track, self-doubt creeps back in and I'm looking at the map again. How many was it this way? Did I count right? I do this until it gives me a headache, and then I give up and decide to sit on a bench and imagine the conversation I'll have to have with Dad when I finally find him in the queue.

I turn on my mobile for the first time since we left the estate, and check the time; I have a few hours before the auditions close. I can't even bear to think what state Dad must be in – him and that king-size duvet with KASSIDY KENNEDY HAS THE X FACTOR painted on it – but the one, two, three, four phone beeps announcing new messages is just a small clue. Five. Six, seven. Eight? Oh no.

There are eight new voicemail messages, from twenty-five calls. There are seven texts that I allow my eyes to graze but don't quite take in: I could have written them myself, after all:

You promised me.

I trusted you.

You are letting me down.

I am hurt.

I am worried.

WHERE ARE YOU?

He's going to be even more furious when he sees what I'm wearing. I look like your (very) average teenager. No 'superstar bling' as he put it. The vaguely drag queen outfit he had in mind is still hanging on the back of my door.

My only consolation is that I'm not even a tiny bit scared of meeting Simon Cowell, if I even get that far, which, knowing my dad, I will (he'll use one of his many resources: puppy-dog eyes, guilt trip, lame joke collection, wallet).

After a while I realise that I am tugging clumps of hair from the nape of my neck. And that this is something I've been doing a lot lately. I freeze, completely freaked out, because I know it's something I do every time I'm stressed, but it's knocking on the door of Things I Do wanting to be let in, wanting to become a normal part of my life. I think back to the leaflet.

Self-harm may become a factor. This can include cutting, burning, hair-pulling and eating disorders.

Is that what's happening here? Could this be the start of becoming the one in ten?

Suddenly this journey seems like the wrong thing to do. But am I just scared of the audition or of my dad or of something even scarier – of my own mind? Of the nameless chemicals that act without known cause and have no cure? I sit down before I fall down, and I pull my sleeve over my hand, bunch it into my fist and exhale into it. The stress moves to my left leg, which becomes possessed by a frantic jiggle. At the sound of a familiar voice I turn to the stairs leading up from the platform. The jiggling stops. I could pick those long legs out of a line-up; they are Izzy's, and she's shouting goodbye to Char.

'Take care, babe!' she calls.

I panic and get up from the bench and face the Tube map again. What am I doing? We've been best friends since we were four. She's so familiar to me I sometimes even forget her name. Does that make sense? Oh, God, do I ever make sense? I need Izzy. And here I am contemplating avoiding her on a Tube platform. I sense her pass.

'Izz.'

'Kass! You gave me a fright. What are you doing here? Shouldn't you . . .?'

'Yep, I should. I'm late. Just on my way now.'

'Right. Well, good luck, babe. I'm off to the other platform. Probably see you . . . Monday, I guess?'

This is awful. It's as if we're reading from the wrong script, and stumbling over the words because they don't feel true to us. I could walk away now, and I wouldn't have to face the resentment I feel because she's just spent the morning with someone who hates me, or the guilt I feel because I know I've been a rubbish friend to her.

'Wait,' I say, grabbing her arm and then feeling like I've invaded her space and letting go. 'Wait. How's things? How's stuff with your parents?' The roar of the Tube wipes out the last half of my sentence.

'Better get your train, Kass.'

'Doesn't matter, I'll get the next one. Let's sit here for a bit.'

'But what about your dad, and the audition?'

'It's OK. Just sit.' I go to the bench and pat a space

next to me. She sits a little further away than where I patted. 'So, the stuff with your parents?'

She breathes out heavily and her wiry frame seems to collapse a bit.

'It's . . . weird,' she says. 'You think you know how things are, and then it all gets turned upside down.'

'I know what you mean,' I say. She smiles politely, but this is not the time to make her see that I really do. 'What does your therapist say?'

'She says I have to let my parents make their own mistakes.'

I chew on that, willing my mind to focus on Izzy's problem instead of relating it to my own. I manage a feeble 'Ironic.' And a shrug.

The Tube roar doesn't have anything to wipe out this time, but we look at each other and I wrinkle my nose and shake my head. When it stops and the doors open I say, 'I'll get the next one.'

'OK, if you're sure,' she says.

'Absolutely.'

The Tube pulls away, and I swallow a lump made entirely of guilt at the thought of my dad still standing in the queue.

'Why didn't you tell me how much this was upsetting you?' I say. 'Char mentioned it.'

'I was going to tell you. I tried to, but other things kept getting in the way and you've just seemed a bit . . . somewhere-else-ish.'

'I know, I'm sorry. So, will you tell me now?' I give her this look that for an instant makes me feel like someone's walked over my grave – and then I realise that it is the look Dad gives me when he wants forgiveness.

'They've been really open about how they feel,' she says. 'They want it to be a new start for all of us, but they're being *really* considerate of *my* feelings . . .'

'That's good, isn't it?'

'It's nauseating, Kass. They're saying they won't get back together if it's going to mess me up.'

For a moment I can't work out why she doesn't just tell them not to and be done with this stress, but then it clicks.

'Oh. So basically it's *all* up to you.'

'Yep. I've been given the opportunity to either total-ly upset their new loved-up plans, which involve Mum singing love songs again and not wanting to stab every man she meets, and Dad losing Miss Carphone Warehouse and trading in the Porsche and picking flowers for my mum in the park, OR totally ruin *my* life by watching them realise it was all a huge mistake because they're still the same two people who can't live together for more than ten minutes without starting World War Three and then tearing each other apart for the second time and playing tug-of-war with me.' Finally, she breathes.

'Wow,' I say, oh-so-helpfully. 'What is wrong with our parents?'

'Yours are OK, aren't they?'

'Not really. No. Not at all.'

'I didn't know.'

'Nor did I, until recently. Anyway, what do you

think you'll do?'

'I don't know. I mean, shouldn't I want my parents to be happy, and together? What's wrong with me?'

'Oh, Izz, there is *nothing* wrong with you. You're brilliant.' I shift along the bench and put my arms around her. 'I'm so sorry for being a crap friend, Izzy. I'll make it up to you.'

'It's OK, Kass.' She laughs, and it's warm and easy. We come apart, but we're sitting close now. 'I know you can get a bit vague when your dad's making you jump through hoops.'

'It's not that, though. Can we go back to yours and I'll tell you about it?'

"Course we can. I'd love that. But what about the audition?'

I think about the leaflet again:

The child is not to blame for the parent's disorder. It is the adults who must be the 'helpers'. Not the kids.

'Come on.' I pull her up and she towers over me, my willowy, beautiful best friend. 'Oh, and Izz, when did you decide to stop calling me Furby?'

'I haven't. Come on, li'l Furby, *wee-tee-kah-wah-tee.*'

'I can't believe you remember Furbish!' I pretend-punch her and we giggle like the children we were when that joke was born.

I don't know if I'm being brave or a coward, but I know that linking arms with my best friend and going to the other platform feels like the right thing to do.

Chapter Twenty-Three

The Blame Factor

It's dark and I'm soaked with the kind of rain that doesn't feel like it's falling but dancing mid-air, tickling the skin on my face and drenching me in secret.

I've taken the short cut, but there's just an empty space where the Stamping Man usually is. I wonder where he goes when he's not here. Who looks after him?

At Izzy's place, hours earlier, I sent a text message to Dad, to say that I wasn't coming to the audition and that I'd explain everything when I saw him back at home. Then at Izzy's I talked and talked, and Izzy talked and talked, and by the end of it we were both sure we'd sorted everything out about our parents, like taking a bowl of spaghetti, untangling it and lining up the stretched-out strands. But now that I'm going back to face them, it's just spaghetti again.

It's eleven o'clock when I walk up the front path, an

hour after my usual curfew, but I figure that as I'm already up to my eyes in trouble, I might as well go completely under. All the way home I tried to put what I've done into words:

I didn't show up at an audition that I never wanted to go to in the first place.

It doesn't sound so bad, put like that, and it's got me all the way to my front door. But the second I walk in the weight of it weaves its way into my lungs, and my heart sinks when I see Dad at the kitchen table. His head is bowed, and he doesn't flinch even when I shut the front door and let my keys clatter on the hall table.

He's wearing a suit. I focus on that in the silence – I didn't see him leave this morning and for all I know he'd been sleeping in those awful ironed jeans that have become his uniform for the last few weeks. The suit somehow makes me all the more sorry to have hurt him. He tried *so hard*, again, and I didn't try at all.

'Hi,' I say. He remains slumped, but moves a little to show that he's heard me. Completely refusing to notice that he has his blingin' trainers on with the suit, I go to the kettle and start to make him a small cup of con-solation – with milk and two heaped sugars. There are Kit-Kats in the tin but that feels too obvious, as if I really thought that he'd be OK if he *had a break*. (What, rather than a breakdown?) I hear him light up a cigarette, and notice that there's a saucer in front of him overflowing with butts. He only ever smokes inside when he's . . .

'Where's Mum?' I say, a tiny bit louder than the gurgle of the kettle.

'On her way back from Maria's.' He repeats Mum's lie flatly, down into his chest as if hypnotised by the purple swirls on his tie. 'One of their girly nights. Raff's staying at a friend's house.'

'Who? Lucas?'

'Possibly.'

So that's that, then – Raff and Lucas are friends again. I helped do that. Even the Cass thing doesn't feel so bad any more. By rights, my shoulders should feel fifty per cent less weighed down, because two out of my four problems are no more. I don't. I'm so weighed down I'm sensing the beginnings of a hump.

I know this version of Dad so well. He is catatonic with disappointment. Over me. He is on his way to Planet Down.

I set the mugs of tea on two of the red vinyl apples and sit next to him.

'Have you eaten?' I say. He briefly glances at the cool-box and nods. I carry on. 'It was cold today. Did you have a coat on?' He shakes his head. 'You should have taken one.' I don't know why I'm saying what I'm saying, so I shut myself up by drinking too-hot tea in tiny slurps that seem deafening in this heavy atmosphere.

Suddenly he scrapes the chair back, chucks his fag packet on the table and starts to leave.

'I'm going to bed,' he says.

'Dad, wait. Don't leave it like this.'

'Like what, Kassidy?'

'Just sit down, please.'

'I'm tired. I haven't got anything to say to you right now.' He stares at me with bloodshot eyes. 'Goodnight.'

I'm lying here, awake, and I don't know how long I've been staring at my lamp, or when I switched it on, or if I've been to sleep at all. Through the skylight I see it's light outside.

I drag myself up, feeling desperately heavy. Everything is hard work: pulling my sweatshirt off the chair and over my head (the chair falls over), putting on my slipper socks (I fall over), picking a face wipe out of the pack to get rid of yesterday's make-up (a whole clump of them come out). Then I stand on my side of the door, wondering what to expect when I go downstairs.

Before I leave I pick the leaflet out of the book and lay it on my desk. Face up. There it is: what we're dealing with in this house. We can't hide it, or hide from it, any more. In my sweatshirt pocket I have Izzy's mum's business card.

Dr Barbara Franklin
BACP (Senior Accredited Member)
UKCP Psychoanalytic Psychotherapist
PGDip Counselling and Interpersonal Skills
Family Therapist

By the bottom of the little flight of stairs that leads to my bedroom I can hear television noise, and I lose my bottle as I picture Dad in his grey tracksuit, flicking channels, smoking, drinking tea. He'll be Somewhere Else, and heading Who Knows Where. Part of me wants to go back upstairs and crawl under the duvet. By a whisker, the part of me that wins is the part that wants to avoid there being two of us in this household who turn to mush when the going gets tough.

I look for Dad in the armchair but he isn't there. Mum's on the sofa. She looks completely knackered. I shudder to think why, only she doesn't look happy.

'Where's Dad?'

'Oh, morning Kass, I didn't see you there.'

'Uh-huh. Where's Dad?'

'He popped out for some milk.'

'Really? He went out?' I rush to the front door. 'Shouldn't someone go with him? What if he has one of those manic attacks? How could you let him go out by himself?' I start to pull off the slipper socks and hunt around for suitable shoes, sobbing and utterly frustrated by how tired I feel and how alone I am in this. *Where are my shoes?*'

'Kass! Calm down, love! He's OK.' She comes towards me and I plunge my feet into the only shoes I can see, which happen to be Dad's ridiculously white trainers.

'How can he be OK?' I push her back from me. 'Don't come near me, I don't want you near me.' Oh God, but I do, I want someone to hold me and let me cry. I want my old, reliable mum.

'Kass, please listen. Your dad is fine. He was upset about the audition but I think he's coming to terms with it, and with how you feel.'

I stop crying and wipe my face with my sleeve.

'Really? How?'

'I don't know, Kass. We can't predict these things. All I can say is that it's not your fault when Dad gets low – and if I've allowed you to believe otherwise then I'm truly, truly sorry.'

I just sniff, and still can't quite bear to look her in the eye. I step out of the shoes.

'Um. OK.'

'If it helps, he's not wearing the grey tracksuit today.' I can tell by her voice that she's smiling. If she thinks she's getting a smile out of me she can think again. 'Come and sit down. Please, Kass. I know I've let you down. I need to talk to you about what to do next.'

I shuffle towards the armchair, my nose and eyes throbbing from the crying, and feel like I'm about to hear the reading of someone's will: *To my daughter, Kassidy, I bequeath a life of twisted lies and cover-ups while I swan off to do despicable things with her best friend's creepy dad.*

'Your dad and I have been talking since last night. I haven't told him yet about Graham but I'm going to.'

'You're *what*? You can't tell him *that*! That'll kill him! Worse, it'll make him go completely nuts. You just can't do it. You can't! Look, I've got Doctor Franklin's card – I was going to give it to Dad, she can get him an appointment with someone. But you can't tell him what you've done – he'll flip and then I'll never convince him to try to get this sorted. Haven't you done enough?'

'Kass, calm down.'

'And *stop* telling me to calm down!'

'Well, I've got to! I'm your mother!' She stands over me; she's finally lost her cool, like she did in Char's kitchen. 'Look, I know I've done this all wrong – I'm not perfect. And I know on the face of it I look like a pretty shit mother and an appalling wife, but I'm trying here, Kass, I am trying to fix things, but I need one thing from you.'

Strangely, I feel calmer. It's a weird kind of 'someone is shouting at me and I needed it' calmer. Except that I'm dreading what it is she needs from me.

'Kass, I need you to go to Raff, explain what's happening here today with me talking to your dad about Graham and how this family goes forward, especially about Dad's health. I need you to spend the day with him – I'll give you money to see a film, eat, do whatever. You're in charge. I need you to look after each other while I deal with Dad, and then I need you to come home. Can you do that?'

I nod.

'Um, are you leaving us?' I sniff.

'Oh no, Kass, no. Darling, I'd never leave you.'

'Are you leaving Dad?'

'No. I'm going to try to sort things out. I mean really try. Is that OK?'

'OK.'

She wants to hug me, I can tell, but I'm not ready, so I edge my way out of the armchair and go up to my room to get ready. I have no idea how Mum thinks that Dad will ever get over this, or that they'll ever be normal again, but somehow this feels better than I thought it would; it feels like the right thing is happening. And I have instructions. Easy ones.

When I come back down, Dad still isn't there.

'A pint of milk, you said.'

'You know what he's like. He's called me to say he decided to drive to Tesco and get a whole load of shopping. Your dad doesn't do things by halves.' The way she says that makes it sound as if she still loves him. But then, how could she be unfaithful? And how could they have done it to me and Char? I feel myself harden again.

'When will I get to explain to him about yesterday?'

'Later. It'll be OK. He understands.' She's firm, she's kind. I could almost like this New Mum. I just wish I didn't still hate her.

On my way out she asks for the business card.

I don't go to Luke's house to collect Raff; the phone calls with Cass were stressful enough without actually running into him. I text Raff and we meet outside the shopping centre. He comes towards me, smiling.

'Everything OK with you and Luke?' I say.

'Yeah. Thanks, Sis. Luke's brother even said I could be a roadie. We had a wicked night listening to the band.'

'Oh, right, so how did they get on at the audition?'
I sound breezy when I say this. Maybe if I sound breezy
I will start to feel breezy. About a decade of hardcore
practice should do it.

'Slated. They got through to Cowell and he called
them average and a bit greasy.'

'Ouch.' This feels weird; kind of like Simon Cowell
has inadvertently defended my honour. 'So, you're a
roadie. And do roadies live on their BlackBerries and
commit credit card fraud?'

'Ha. Maybe I'll break the mould. Anyway, what are
we doing here?'

'We need to talk.'

'Oh. Is it about Mum and Dad?'

'They don't call you a Pint-Sized Evil Genius for
nothing. Come on, I'll buy you a coffee.'

'I don't drink coffee.'

'Tea, then.'

'Nope.'

'Chicken soup.'

'Hilarious.'

'OK, how about a hazelnut hot chocolate with
whipped cream and marshmallows and a double chocolate muffin to go with it?'

'Now you're talking.'

So my brother and I go to get high on sugar and talk
about our messed-up family. Only, before long, Raff
seems to lose interest in brooding about what might
happen, and instead he starts talking about the past.
Fun stuff we've all done together – holidays and

random Saturdays – when Dad hasn't been at either end of the pendulum. Things I'd forgotten. In fact, when he starts it's as if he's talking about a completely different family. He even makes it sound as if he and I get on. I sound quite good in his stories. Most of them, anyway. We're getting along better than we have in years when a text comes.

'It's from Mum.' My finger hovers over the button.

'Well, read it, then!'

'I'm scared to.'

'Kass, it'll be fine. Look, they're the adults, we're just the kids – it's not our job to fix everything or blame ourselves for everything. We've got enough going on, haven't we? Just in normal life?'

'Who made you so clever all of a sudden?' I say to my Rat-Faced Mutant Little Brother, who, I now realise, I wouldn't be without for anything in the world. He looks pretty happy.

The text says:

Coast clear. We've talked. Dad has gone to a friend's but he's OK.
Don't worry. Come home.

All the way home I do the opposite of what Mum said: I worry. I worry about Dad's state of mind, and about which friend he's gone to – I can't think of any good friends that Dad would turn to over something like this. He's always said he didn't need friends; he had Mum.

Raff automatically uses the shortcut and I'm too caught up in my thoughts to say otherwise, though when we pass the Stamping Man my worry just about trebles. Is *he* someone's dad? How did he start out? Healthy and happy, or was he always like that, always afflicted by the nameless chemicals that attack at random and for which there is no cure? And is my dad standing in the street somewhere, alone and going mad?

Mum opens the door when we're halfway up the path and Raff runs into her arms. I manage a smile, but once she's promised me another hundred times that Dad's really OK – it turns out he's with Tony Ferrari of all people – I just want to be alone.

– *I'm waiting.*

– *For what, Mr Cowell?*

– *An apology, that's what. I thought we had a date yesterday.*

– *Yeah, sorry about that, I had a better offer.*

– *Charming.*

– *Oh, come on, you only wanted me to come so you could show off a few of those pre-packaged barbed comments. I can hear them now: 'Utterly, utterly average', 'You've got the personality of a candle', 'If you're a singer, I'm Tweety Pie'.*

– *You know, I like you less and less.*

– *I'm not so bad. And I am sorry I couldn't make it to see you. There's just a lot going on now, and chasing someone else's dream isn't at the top of the list.*

– *Very profound. But point taken; I suppose you have*

had a lot on your plate. You did the right thing.
– Wow, you almost sound nice.
– I am nice!
– Yeah, you're OK, Mr Cowell.
– You're OK too, Kass Kennedy.

Chapter Twenty-Four

Let's Face The Music, And Duck

Four days later, I catch two buses to Tony Ferrari's house. On the first bus I cast my mind back a few weeks and wonder what I'd have thought if someone had told me I'd be on my way to visit my dad – who'd left home because my mum had confessed to an affair with my best friend's father – at the home of a Simon Cowell impersonator.

On the second bus I rehearse over and over what I'll say to Dad about leaving him stranded at the audition. I can't really think about what to say about everything else until we've got past that.

Tony Ferrari lives in a new-build estate that looks like Legoland, without the cool little people with yellow heads. All the window frames and front doors are bright blue, and each house has two pointy dark green plants either side of the path. There's nothing to tell them apart, but I spot Tony's house a mile off because the number plate on his car says S1MON 2.

My dad opens the door. He is unshaven and has dark circles under his eyes, but he smiles and we hug on the doorstep for ages.

'Come in,' he says. 'Tony's gone out to give us some space.'

We step over several pizza boxes to reach the kitchen, which is supremely bare except for brown rings of tea on nearly every surface and about fifteen unwashed mugs in the sink. Dad suddenly turns round and says, 'I should have made lunch. Do you want lunch? I can ring for pizza.' He picks up the phone and starts to dial.

'No, Dad!' I take it off him. 'I don't want to eat. I came to talk.'

'Right.'

'Let's sit down,' I say.

He actually does. I don't want to get giddy with power but I think this is the first time he's done something I've asked.

He combs his hands through his (seriously unwashed) hair, and then he starts to look twitchy, like something's brewing, working its way out of him, about to explode, and then he gets up again and smacks his hand on the table.

'*Why* didn't you come? *Why?*'

I'm scared, and try not to look at the bead of spit in the corner of his mouth.

'Dad, please.'

'Please *what*? I waited and waited for you.' He is bright red and standing over me. 'I looked like an idiot. How could you do that to me?' All I can see are his bloodshot eyes.

'Just listen to me for once!' I face him head-on, but my voice is shaking.

'No, you listen to me, Kassidy. I was there for hours in that queue. I never thought you'd let me down like that – *ever*.' He starts to pace around, miming with his hands as if he's clutching each word, flinging it down, reaching for another, swiping it out of his way. 'I got to the front, *finally*, and do you know what I said to them? *Nothing*. I waited in that queue in silence most of the night and all day, in *silence*, and when I made it to the desk I said *nothing*. I just turned round and walked back out.' He looks at me, getting out of breath, and starts to light a cigarette but can't quite coordinate himself, so he throws the packet across the room. 'Do you have any idea how that felt? A thirty-nine-year-old man struck dumb. I was humiliated! I felt like . . . *nothing*.'

I don't know why I thought I could do this. I'm already crying. I don't say a word, just stand and face him. What he's saying doesn't even sound like a huge deal – he was in a queue, so what? He got to the end and said nothing, so what? But there is so much more to this. Mum said he was dealing with it and with everything else, but she must have got it wrong. I'm scared.

But then he slumps in his chair like a puppet with his strings cut. When he speaks again his voice is completely different, low and calm, as if he's playing multiple characters in a play.

'There were thousands there,' he says. 'People with tents; whole families; such a collection of people I've never seen before. It wasn't like the other auditions we've been to. People dressed up in silly costumes, people practising their songs in the open air, chatting to one another, waving to the cameras. They were all buzzing. And the more I saw how much they all wanted it, the more I realised how little you do.' He sounds so bitter as he looks up at me. 'That's true, isn't it?'

Even the gods of sarcasm would frown on me for taking this opportunity, so I simply say, 'Yes, it's true.'

He looks away again, but this time his shoulders judder and he cries. It's just for a second, but it's awful.

'I sat on the cool-box and waited for you, shifting along as the queue moved. I must have overheard a hundred conversations between parents and their teenagers. *Do you think I'll get to sing in front of the real judges, Dad? Will you come in with me, Dad? Can we go through the songs one more time, Dad? Oh, Dad, I'm so nervous!*' He's doing impressions of these kids, in that animated way of his, and I have to bite the inside of my mouth – I feel sick and hysterical at once.

'At first I thought, that'll be me and Kassidy soon, when she gets here. But then I heard *your* voice in my head: *I don't want to go, Dad. Leave me alone, Dad. I'm only doing this one last time so you'll stop making me, Dad.* That's what you say, isn't it?'

'Dad, you know it is. I've always said it.'

'Yes, yes, I know.'

I'm about to speak but I realise that for all his ranting a minute ago he's actually worked it out for himself.

He looks at me again, and this time I know he's not playing any new character; he's not Dad the Game Show Host, or Dad the Disappointed Parent, or Dad the Cheeky, Charming Child, or even Moody Dad from Planet Down. He's my real dad, the one I knew was buried underneath all that – the dad I put up with all the other dads for.

'You don't want to be a star, do you?'

I shake my head, and allow just a tiny smile.

'You just want to make your own mind up.'

I think it's a rhetorical question.

'You want your old Dad to butt out.'

'Maybe just a bit,' I say.

He empties his lungs purposefully. Then he rests one arm on the table, the rest of his body slack, his head too heavy for his neck.

'I was doing it for me,' he says, his voice a quiet scraping sound. 'When I was ten, my father . . .' His face crumples so that I know what the next word is. But he uncrumples himself and tries again. 'My father died, Kass.' He clears his throat and shifts away as if he knew I was going to reach for him. Tears are streaming down his face, but he's completely still; he just lets them fall. 'He was . . . a very brave man. Firefighter.' He laughs a hollow laugh. 'Classic hero, right?'

I don't think he wants me to say anything. I am so afraid of what he's about to tell me. I feel like it shouldn't just be me here.

'I never measured up. 'Course I didn't! Look at me.'
He shifts his legs and then his arms, as if he's showing
me how defective he is. 'My mother took it very badly;
it was like she couldn't wait to join him, and the only
thing keeping her here was me. She resented me for
that, I think.' He stops. Sobs: 'Hated me, even.'

'But she was your mum,' I say. It feels like a stupid
thing to have said, but it is so hard to watch my dad
sitting there, his face wet with tears and snot, like a little
boy.

'It was hard for her, Kassidy.' He sniffs and wipes his
whole face with his sleeve, looks at how gross it is now
and hides it under the table. 'She loved my dad and, try
as I might, I was nothing like him. Nothing I ever did
was good enough. When I was sixteen – the day after
my birthday, it was – she kicked me out. "Take your
stuff, and don't come back until you've made something
of yourself. Make your dad proud." She said I'd thank
her one day.'

He goes quiet and stares into space. But I can't let
him stop now.

'And did you? Thank her?' I'm trying not to let it
show in my voice that I think his mum sounds
horrible.

He gets up and walks to the sink.

'Didn't have the chance, Kassidy.'

'Oh.'

He's hunched over.

'How did she die?' I say, because I can't think what

else to do except ask stupid questions.

'She didn't,' he says, standing up straight and looking back at me briefly. 'I went back five years later and she'd gone. Moved, I mean. No address. No message.'

'Well, maybe she tried to contact you but she couldn't find you, Dad. Maybe—'

'No, Kassidy,' he says, firmly. 'I think I knew, even that first day I left, that I'd never see her again. She wanted rid of me. I wasn't good enough. She's still out there, Kassidy, not wanting to know me because I'm . . . still . . . nothing.'

'Dad! Don't say that!'

'It's OK, Kassidy – I'm OK. I'll drag myself back up – always do. I'm just thinking aloud.'

I wish I knew what to do. Suddenly this huge chunk of Dad's history is here in the room, and it explains so much, but it's too big to take in.

'Forty, Kass. I'm nearly forty. And what have I got to show for it?'

I open my mouth to defend him and his life, but I think he's going to answer it himself, looking out into the neat square garden, or more likely looking at his own reflection in it.

'I've got two wonderful children. And I *did* have a wonderful wife. But I ruined that, too.'

'No, Dad, that's not fair.' I get up and go to him, try to wrap my arms around him from the side.

'What shall I do, Kassidy?' He looks me in the eye.

'Come home, Dad.'

Chapter Twenty-Five

Two Sandwiches Short of a Picnic

This is me, imagining my parents arguing at the kitchen table; still round, still with the red vinyl apples, only everything else is different now.

This is me; this is how I am. It is Saturday night but there's no pizza – who'd have thought I'd ever miss that painful little ritual? I'm in my bedroom with a family bag of Wotsits, a bottle of Sprite and four Tim-Tams (Mum's been guilt-shopping again). It's OK, I'm going to take up running soon. Preferably far away from this place.

Joke.

There's an irritating smooshing against the door. I'm secretly glad it's Raff but I can't let the side down (the side being all bad-tempered older sisters), so I say 'What?' It's not really a question, but an expression of how unwelcome he is.

'I'm hungry. You've got all the food,' he says. I try to lick the evidence off my fingers but they are stained orange.

'OK, come in.'

Raff lies stomach-down on my bed and puts an entire Tim-Tam in his mouth.

'That's gross,' I say. His reply is very crumby. Then he puts his chocolaty mouth on the Sprite bottle and glugs. I make the appropriate face. It's difficult to believe that this model of sophistication, now belching loudly, is the same one who nearly got mixed up in a gang of crims. Bless him, little sod. He still carries his BlackBerry everywhere, and seems to have more money than any thirteen-year-old should. But I know he's OK. We talk now.

'What are they arguing about?' I say.

'Dad put an empty margarine tub back in the fridge.'

'Are you kidding?'

'Err, *yes*. What do you *think* they're arguing about, Kass? Dumb question.'

Oh. It's nice that I have taught my little brother one thing: sarcasm.

'But what specifically?' I say.

'He's asking her what your mate's dad's got that he hasn't got.'

'And what's she saying?'

'"Paul, can't we just talk about us instead of him? That's over."'

'Is that supposed to be an impression of Mum? That sucks.'

'Whatever. Can I have another Tim-Tam?'

I hand him one and wipe the Sprite bottle with my sleeve before taking a swig.

'So, what's happening with you?' I ask. He shrugs. 'Raff, if you're going to spend the evening in my room you have to actually talk to me.'

'All right. Umm . . . I got picked for the football team.'

'Yeah? That's brilliant. Did you tell Dad?'

'Yep.'

'What did he say?'

'He said good.'

'OK. Good.'

'Yep.' He pretends not to be too bothered, but I know different now, and I've got to do my bit to get them closer together. 'Hey Kass, remember that time I blacked out the TV screen with marker pen and told Mum and Dad it was you?'

'Raff, are you going to make a long list of confessions now that I've helped you out and you like me again? Because I've got a long memory.' I smile at him.

'Just that one. Sorry.' He's smiling, too. Idiot. Loveable idiot.

'What else is happening?'

'Err . . . I dunno, when are we doing that family therapy stuff?'

'Next week.'

'Is it gonna be weird? I don't want to do anything weird.'

'I think she's just going to lock us in a tiny room and

release hundreds of spiders into it.'

'*What?*'

For a smart little boy he sure is gullible.

'Joke. It's just going to be talking and stuff. *Feeeeelings.* You know those? I think you've got one somewhere, buried deep, deep down.'

He turns the Wotsit packet upside down over his mouth and gets orange dust in his eyes. When he's restored his vision he says:

'Are we gonna have to talk about "Graham"?' He says 'Graham' with a fairly decent robot voice and does robot hands to go with it.

'Maybe. They're moving, you know. Him and Char. Izzy told me.'

'Oh, right. Hey, have you finished the Tim-Tams?'

Brothers.

Raff starts to listen to my Mp3 player, pulling a face every time he flicks to a new song. Then his face relaxes and he flips onto his back. It's sort of nice to have him here, even if he's no good at gossip and hasn't noticed that he has a blob of chocolate on the end of his nose.

I log on to MSN. Stix isn't there, and that's probably a good thing. He's sent me a few nice texts but I'm trying to keep my distance until all the fuzzy feelings are gone. Then *maybe* we can be friends. He messed up that night but I'm OK; it's the end of us but it's not the end of everything. It's getting easier to think that he's a good guy who made a mistake. Confession: there was even a tiny part of me that wondered if we could be more than friends, but where do you go when the beginning of a relationship is so difficult? Maybe if you've been together for years, and your life together is so tangled up, you can move on – like Mum and Dad say they're trying to – but I'm too young to compromise.

The only person online is Char. We haven't spoken since the karaoke night, except for the time that Mum and I had to drag Dad away from her front door and she said, coldly: 'Just go.' And I replied, 'Sorry,' and held up my sobbing father while he promised to do all sorts of violent things to 'Graham'.

I should think of what I want to say before I type a word, but that might make me lose my nerve.

curlygirl: hello, do you want to talk?
char: about what?
curlygirl: how sorry I am?
char: how sorry are you?
curlygirl: big time. I never meant to hurt you.
char: I know.
curlygirl: I did kiss him at first, I shouldn't have. And then it got a bit scary. It was my fault, I'm really sorry.
char: Izzy told me everything. Not exactly a Dream Boy, was he? I'm sorry too.
curlygirl: You are? What for?
char: Being a total nutjob. It wasn't so much about that. Well, it was and it wasn't.
curlygirl: Yeah I know. What I don't get is why you didn't tell me what was going on.

curlygirl: Char?

char: Yep, well that's the screwed-up bit. The whole reason I found out was because Dad had stopped grounding me for having a hair out of place, etc etc. He seemed happy, and I got suspicious. I overheard him on the phone.

curlygirl: No way – that's how I found out. God, aren't they idiots?

char: Tell me about it. So anyway, half of me was like totally furious, and the other half didn't want Dad to get hurt again like he did when my mum left. She was – your mum, I mean – a really good influence on him.

I sit back in my chair and look at those words: *a really good influence*. I don't think I've ever known Mum to influence Dad until recently; in fact that's what used to wind me up so much.

curlygirl: That's weird. To be honest I don't really want to think about it any more.

char: Me neither.

. . .

char: Our place is up for sale.

curlygirl: Yeah, I know.

char: But we're not moving that far away after all. Dad doesn't want me to switch schools when we've got our exams next year. He asked me what I thought, about going to school with you and stuff – that's the first time he's ever asked me what I thought.

curlygirl: Well?

char: well what?

curlygirl: Well what do you think about going to school with me?

curlygirl: if you could answer a tiny bit quicker that would really help how sick and nervous I feel over here.

char: I guess it'll be weird. Doesn't feel weird on here though.

curlygirl: Yeah, I know. Maybe we could start with MSN and slowly build ourselves up to a real-life conversation.

char: Sounds good.

curlygirl: ☺ Better not tell my dad though. He's really screwed up. But we're all going to do therapy. We've been Izzy-fied ☺

char: think I might avoid telling mine too.

curlygirl: hey we'll be like Romeo and Juliet.

char: oh god, don't remind me, I haven't even started my essay.

curlygirl: rebel.

char: ☺

curlygirl: ☺

It's about midnight and there's dribble on my pillow – Raff has dozed off. It might be the stress of my home life, or the amount of additives I've consumed this evening, but I'm not even close to tired so I tiptoe downstairs for a change of scene and more supplies.

On the way down I hear Dad snoring in their bedroom. (I think it's still accurate to refer to it as theirs.)

It's good that he's asleep – since Mum confessed, the whole time he's awake it's painful to watch him. He swings from horrible, sad self-deprecation to unbelievable meanness, then regret, then cringe-making showiness, all in the space of five minutes, while Mum stands by totally dignified. A few weeks ago I'd have thought she was being cold and unfeeling, but now I know that this is just the only way to deal with Dad – just let him go through it all until he comes out the other side. Hopefully once we've been to therapy a few times we'll find out new ways of coping. The strangest thing is, even with all this going on, he hasn't gone back to Planet Down – it's weird how it hasn't sent him over the edge. I guess it's not in our control after all. It really is those nameless chemicals and not some rational thing we can contain.

The spare duvet is crumpled on the sofa. Every morning Mum hides it away before we get up, as if we're that stupid. It seems weird that she'd want to protect us from the fact that they're sleeping in different rooms when we already know what's happened and Dad mentions it approximately seven times an hour.

It sounds like she's unpacking the dishwasher.

'Hi,' I say from the doorway.

'Oh hi, Kass. I thought you'd be asleep.'

'I was hungry.'

I take an apple from the fruit bowl – surely that cancels out at least one Tim-Tam – and sit at the table. This is the first time we've been alone since the night of the disco; not that she hasn't tried to make it happen before, but I haven't let her. I'm not saying I've forgiven her now – I still feel like she betrayed me and Raff as well as Dad – but I understand her better. It wasn't just her. It didn't happen because my mum's a cow.

I hope everyone knows how wise I am these days. Ha. Izzy would be proud, though she's been busy lately with her dysfunctional-turned-sweetheart parents and her new therapist. She decided she needed a new one. I don't really know how it all works, but I guess I'll find out.

Strange, I've been so scared of losing everything – and of Dad losing IT – that I've barely realised what I've gained. I've got my little brother back and it feels like I could have Mum back, too. In a new and better way. That's why I'm sitting here, I suppose, watching her clean the kitchen, watching her carrying on instead of cracking up, watching her and wondering how I never really saw her before.

'I'm making tea,' she says. I expect she doesn't ask whether I want any because the last time she asked I told her to stick her tea up her . . .

'Yes please,' I say.

One Year Later

Chapter Twenty-Six

I Have A Dream, A Song To Sing

Here I am, Kass Kennedy, one in a million – that is, one average-looking, tone-deaf girl in a queue of a million people waiting to audition for *The X Factor*. Yes! Me! OK, so a million might be a slight exaggeration – a year later I'm still no better at maths. I even doodled my brain falling out of my head on my GCSE exam paper. Dad would be so proud.

He doesn't know I'm here. I thought about telling him, but he's not ready for it yet – he's come a long way, my dad, but it would be the equivalent of blowing cigarette smoke in his face and crowing *ner-ner-ner-ner-ner* (he gave those up, too – I can't say which was harder for him but at least you can buy nicotine patches . . . he had to go cold turkey on the pushy parent stuff).

Let's get one thing straight: I'm not here because I think I've got the X Factor. As if! I'm still just normal, ordinary Kass. Doing this is symbolic. I don't even care how stupid that sounds. Maybe I'm high on audition queue fumes: the heady pollution of all these hopefuls, and knowing that I can enjoy this for what it is. I have zero expectations.

We're passing the time by having a heated debate about what to sing. We're *that* prepared.

'OK, so we've narrowed it down to "Dancing Queen" or "Girls Just Wanna Have Fun",' I say. '*Or* the weird song that Izzy's boyfriend wrote for her.' I know I'm being cheeky, but I also know I can be with my best friends.

'It's not *weird*,' says Izzy. 'Is it, Char?'

'Weird is a bit strong; we just don't know it, Izz, that's all. It's a great song, but maybe not for today.' Sometimes it's really hard to believe that Char was ever *not* this nice. Izzy's boyfriend is a metalhead and the 'love song' he wrote her sounds like someone having their tonsils removed without anaesthetic, and contains the phrases *I am your slave* and *Come to my lair through the catacombs*. Cute.

'Fine,' says Izzy, 'but we're not singing "Dancing Queen" – it's a well-known fact that no one can sing that except Abba. It's physically impossible, even for good singers.'

'True, but do we care?' says Char. 'You want to be a therapist, I want to be a doctor, and Kass wants to have a column in a magazine where she can bitch about life in a *very* sarcastic manner. None of us actually want to get through. Right, Kass?'

'Right, but I really, really want to audition in front

of Simon,' I say. 'So we need to pass this first bit or we won't get to meet him.'

'What is it with you and Simon Cowell? Do you fancy him or what?' says Izzy.

'About as much as I fancy walking over hot coals. Anyway, if I wanted someone who looked like him I could just get it on with my dad's best mate.'

'Uuurgh, Furby, that's gross. Is your dad *still* trying to launch Tony whatshisname?'

'Ferrari. Yep. He's even set up this new company called Looky Likey. Tony's his only client so far. It's a bit sad, but you know my dad. At least I'm not on his client list. Anyway, they're great friends. Like brothers. It's kind of sweet.'

'Aww, yeah, it is sweet,' says Char.

'Interesting,' says Izzy, probably jotting it down in her imaginary therapists' notebook.

'I just . . . I really *like* Simon Cowell,' I say, as if this is news even to me. 'And I want to do this one crazy thing to mark the fact that we're all still best friends even though . . . *you know*, there was all the weird stuff but now it's all cool and . . . OK, am I getting too mushy?'

'Mushy's good,' says Char. 'Although by the looks of this queue we have about a month to decide what to sing. I can't believe how many people are here. Hey, do you know whether, um, Cassian and his band are coming this year?'

This is progress. It took Char and me about six months to stop referring to Cass as 'Whatsisname'.

More recently he's been upgraded to 'Um, Cassian'. Not that we talk about him much, but somehow he and I managed to stay friends – the kind of friend you don't speak to all the time, but when you do it feels like you never stopped. Who'd have thought?

'Didn't Simon Cowell call him "smelly and tone-deaf" last year?' says Izzy.

'I think it was "greasy and distinctly average", actually,' I say. 'Anyway, he's busy up in Manchester with his nerdy degree and gigging in some uni bars.'

'You still hear from him, then.' Izzy's voice is flat and deeply disapproving. She wouldn't give Cass the time of day if he saved her from a burning building, out of loyalty to me. I love her for it; I'd be the same if it had happened to her. 'Doesn't Joe mind?'

Joe . . . Joe . . . rings a vague bell. OK, OK, Joe's my boyfriend. This is all a bit new so excuse me if I blush several shades of scarlet, wear a dumb grin and start giggling. It's not my fault!

'Joe is absolutely fine with it,' I say, using every muscle in my face not to beam at my interrogator. The girls both go *Awwww* and rub my arms as if I'm a playful pup. *Ahem, pull yourself together, Kass!*

'OK, back to business. The audition: the reason we're standing here in this ridiculous queue. The way I see it, we either have to be unbelievably bad – which is quite some skill if you check out some of the people here – or we have to be a bit good, which we could be if Izzy and I sing like mice and you really belt it out, Char.'

'Hmm, I'll do my best, Furbs,' she says. (Did I also fail to mention that use of the nickname had spread like an evil virus?) 'And if Izzy gets her legs out, and you make a few biting remarks, we might actually do it.'

So we decide on 'Girls Just Wanna Have Fun'. We huddle together and sing into the tops of our bottles of water. I can't say I feel relaxed, but this nervy, cloud-nine buzz is just from the thought of laying all this to rest, finally, and because I'm with my best friends who know everything about me and still, somehow, want to stick around.

We've done it.

I'm so excited, a really tiny part of me wants to call my dad and tell him I passed the first stage, but that would be cruel, and I don't need his approval on this – that's not what this is for.

'I can't believe they put us through,' says Char.

'I know, are we so bad we're good, or so good we don't know it?' says Izzy.

'I don't care. This is brilliant,' I say. They both look at me and smile. I feel really young and silly, and good about that.

People are coming out of the judges' room crying, and we've made a pact never to make a joke about them. But everyone else is open to abuse (quietly). And to be fair, we also make jokes about each other in between.

'What about him,' whispers Izzy, 'Looks like he ironed his jeans. Isn't that illegal?'

'My dad used to iron his,' I say. 'But he's been rehabilitated now. Ooh, look at her with the thong up round her armpits and the jeans halfway down her hips.'

'Nasty,' says Char. 'Hang on – look at *him*.'

'Yeah, he's nice,' I say. And we look at each other. 'You have him.'

'Nah.'

'What do you mean, nah? He's hot!'

Char shrugs and tries to hide a smile.

'Charlotte, you tell me this minute what that smile is about!'

'I have absolutely no idea what you . . . OK! But you promise not to laugh?'

'Cross our hearts,' says Izzy, and we both clamp our hands over our mouths.

'Right. There's a new family on our street and one of the boys is really really cute. New Dream Boy!'

'You're kidding – what is it about your street? It's like the local council are using it as a dumping ground for fit blokes,' I say. 'So, does Dream Boy have a name?'

Char swanks around a bit and then says:

'He has a name, a phone number and a date next week!'

The three of us squeal like guinea pigs until a voice says:

'30786.'

My heart skips a beat.

'That's us,' I say. 'I can't do it.'

'30786?'

'Oh yes you can, Furbs,' says Izzy. 'You're brave. You're brilliant.'

'We're with you, Kass,' says Char.

'30786? Are you 30786?' says a frazzled girl with a clipboard.

'Yes,' I say. I stand up; my legs are like jelly. 'That's us.'

'Come this way, please, girls. Simon is waiting.'

Acknowledgements

In this book are more than just my own fingerprints, and I'd like to thank in particular: my agent Louise Burns, my editor Imogen Cooper, my friend Caroline Green and the 'Anonymous Reader' at Hilary Johnson's Author's Advisory Service, for their wonderful insights. Thank you to the very talented team at Chicken House, the wits at MsB, and those at WW who gave great feedback. Thank you to Sascha, Ruth and Kellie for true friendship, and to Dan Box for timely kicks up the rear. Thanks to my supportive parents, Sue and Chris Gale. And finally thank you to Aaron, for always knowing when I need to go back to the Shire.

'Other Side of the World' by K T Tunstall, is from her album 'Eye to the telescope'.

Every effort has been made to trace or contact all copyright holders. The publishers would be please to rectify any errors or omissions brought to their notice, at the earliest opportunity.